Hi Carolyn!
Thanks f...
Lov...

Pasta Mike

Andrew Cotto (signature)

A Novella about Friendship & Loss

Andrew Cotto

Black Rose Writing | Texas

The author grants the final approval for this literary
material.

First printing

This is a work of fiction. Names, characters, businesses,
places, events, and incidents are either the products of the
author's imagination or used in a fictitious manner. Any
resemblance to actual persons, living or dead, or actual
events is purely coincidental.

ISBN: 978-1-68433-865-8
PUBLISHED BY BLACK ROSE WRITING
www.blackrosewriting.com

Printed in the United States of America
Suggested Retail Price (SRP) $16.95

Pasta Mike is printed in Book Antiqua

*As a planet-friendly publisher, Black Rose Writing does its best to
eliminate unnecessary waste to reduce paper usage and energy
costs, while never compromising the reading experience. As a result,
the final word count vs. page count may not meet common
expectations.

This book is dedicated to:

Tina, Jack, Carly, and Colin O'Shea: This is for you
most of all.

Mike's beloved siblings and their families.

The legions of Mike's "best friends" who miss him
every day.

Finally: To Judy Goldstein, my sister in suffering and
the one who knows best what it's like to lose such a
friend. Here's to Karen and Mike in heaven!

Thanks to Talkspace for commissioning the essay that inspired this book.

Thanks to Diane Roncone for the editing and counsel.

Thanks to Allison Arevalo of Pasta Louise for inspiring the title (and for the pasta!).

Thanks to everyone at Black Rose Writing.

Pasta Mike

One of my favorite memories of Mike O'Shea was the night we ate at Per Se. We were celebrating our 40th birthdays, and the choice of restaurant was my idea. I knew Mike had never heard of Per Se, as he had zero interest in New York's fine dining experiences. Massive and Irish, Mike was a meat and potatoes guy. A special occasion for him was usually at a steakhouse or a family-style Italian joint, but I'd become a food snob thanks to a generous expense account in a previous career, and I'd been dying to go to Per Se—considered one of the best restaurants in America—since it opened, which was after I'd entered the decidedly non-expense account profession of being a teacher and a writer. Our 40th birthdays seemed like a good excuse to splurge. All I had to do was run it by Mike, so I did.

"Whatever you want, And," he said. "Whatever you want."

My birth name is Andrew. People called me Andy growing up, but Mike referred to me as "And" as if there was a need for him to have a name for me that no one else used. He kept calling me that as we got older and even into adulthood, even after I started using the name "Andrew" to seem more mature. I loved that he called me "And" — especially since it was often tagged onto the end of a sentence that demonstrated not only our special bond but Mike's graciousness. Both our bond and Mike's graciousness would be on full display the night we would celebrate together at Per Se. Unfortunately, it would be the last time that such blessings would ever be enjoyed.

•   •   •

I like to think that Mike and I knew each other before we were born. I don't mean this in a spiritual way or in some other universe. I believe this because our mothers were pregnant with us during the same summer of 1968, and our families lived around the corner from each other in our section of Queens. It was the kind of neighborhood nobody was forbidden from entering or passing through, a fairly quiet working-class enclave of mostly Irish and Italian families. The Irish were there first, then came the Italians. I understand there was some beef back in the day, but by the summer Mike and I were born, harmony prevailed and marriages formed between some Irish boys and Italian girls and Italian boys and Irish girls. There were also some Greek families and Jewish families, and newly arrived immigrants from the Caribbean and Central America, too. It was all good and a great place to grow up, no more so for me and Mike; we had it made.

Mike's family was all Irish, and we were 100 percent Italian. Mike was the youngest of five kids, and I had an older brother and a lot of cousins who lived nearby. Mike's dad served and protected on behalf of the New York Police Department; my father was part-owner of a manufacturing plant that made vinyl albums and audio cassettes for record companies. Both of our mothers, like most mothers around at the time, stayed home and kept the house, though my mother had the help of her mother who lived with us throughout my childhood and adolescence.

My mother and Mike's didn't know each other that well until they realized each was pregnant and due around the same time, so with that in common, they started getting together to talk about their pregnancies, taking turns visiting each other's stoops in the late afternoon, before they had to get dinner on the table. Mike's mom had almost 10 years on my mom, but they got along well and remained friends after having their sons five days apart that summer. We were even baptized together, the only two babies to take the holy water that day at St. Catherine's Church. Mike's mother and my mother took their newborns for walks together in strollers and then to the park where Mike and I would take our first steps.

My earliest memories are of being on the floor with Mike, in the living room of one of our houses, the sounds of our mothers chatting and the smell of the cigarettes they smoked. Mike and I were on the floor, practically tangled, trying to use our limbs to stay upright. That sense of togetherness lasted throughout childhood as we grew into kids who could navigate playgrounds together or glide on swing sets side by side. I remember the weird sense of separation when we both started school, Mike going to the Catholic school his mother drove him to in their station wagon and me holding my mother's hand as we walked to the public school that was only a few blocks away.

My next memories are when we are somewhat older, still kids but independent enough to go outside on our own, maybe 2nd or 3rd grade. We weren't the only kids around. There were tons of kids—our age, younger, and older—but I always met up with Mike before doing anything else. I'd be home from school first, so I'd wait on my stoop until Mike and his mother drove by in their station wagon with paneled sides, and then I'd go around the corner, still dressed in the clothes I wore to school, and wait until Mike had time to change out of his school uniform and have a snack of boxed cookies or cakes his mother always had on hand. I'd climb the smooth, wide, concrete steps of Mike's family's row house—one of those with the facades in front that barreled out, just like all the others down the tree-lined, one-way block they lived on. Their house, and their whole block, was nicer than the vinyl and brick A-frames where we lived, with different families on each floor, but that recognition or distinction or whatever meant nothing to me or anyone else around. We were all equals.

When I climbed up the steps, there would be noise from Mike's siblings from the living room or yelling down the stairs, and I'd wait for a moment of quiet before ringing the doorbell. I'd listen for the sound of Mike's mom coming from the kitchen and see her shadow against the wall as she came to the door to begin the familiar exchange.

"Oh, Andy," she would say, as if she were surprised to see me. "And how are you?"

"Good," I'd say. "Is Mike home?"

"I'll check," she'd respond and then inspect me for a minute, wiping her hands on the front of her apron. "And how's your mother?"

"She's good," I'd say, peeking past her apron-wrapped waist and into the house.

"Wait here," she'd tell me and disappear back inside, closing the front door but not all the way.

Around a minute later Mike would come to the door wearing hand-me-down clothes from his brothers, patched dungarees, shirts having something to do with sports, and canvas sneakers. He'd step onto the stoop and nod, something he'd learned from his big brothers, and then he'd hold out his open right hand and I'd pop it with the fist of my left. And we'd be off.

There were so many places to go, all within a handful of blocks, and all those blocks were watched over by the shop owners or the adults going about their business or the grandmothers sitting in the windows, staring at the streets. Our first stop was always the schoolyard, where the Olympics of city sports would basically be going on every day: stickball, basketball, street hockey, touch football. We did them all with whoever needed players when we arrived. Sometimes we'd split up and play different games; sometimes we'd be on different teams. It didn't matter.

On other days, if it was raining or cold or no one was really around for whatever reason, we'd go to the strip where all the stores were, to the pizzeria for slices and squares, and to play video games like Asteroids and Pac-Man. There were bakeries and Italian Ice places, and a bar, Brady's Irish Haven, where Mike's uncle would be just inside the front door or out front in a lawn chair talking about horse races with his pals and filling out forms.

I think of it now like it was kind of magical, and I guess it was—a safe paradise of freedom and games and adventure—but what made it so special for me was that I had a friend with me the whole time. He was always there; my constant companion. And I was thinking about that as my wife and I were on our way to meet Mike and his date to celebrate the 40th birthdays of friends who were friends since before they were born.

• • •

My wife's name is Lauren, but she goes by Laurie with her parents and with those who know her outside of work. She has blonde hair and squared shoulders, perfect posture, all back from her days growing up as a competitive gymnast. I met her when I was at Fairfield College in Connecticut and she attended the state's university. Laurie's cousin, who lived in the same town as her in Nassau County, Long Island, was my friend at Fairfield, and I'd hitch rides to New York on occasion when Laurie would swing through on her way down from UConn to pick up her cousin to go home for long weekends or longer breaks.

I thought she was so gorgeous; nice, and interesting, too. Their family owned a pub in Manhasset, where they lived, and you could tell that Laurie had been a waitress and bartender for many years in her take-no-shit attitude, especially from men, that served her well in the financial sector she went into after graduating. When we first met, I flirted with her like crazy, back and forth to and from New York to Connecticut, and she tolerated my attempts at charm with just enough encouragement to sustain my effort, though there was always the casual reference to "my boyfriend" or "the guy I'm seeing…" who always seemed to be an athlete of some sort: hockey or lacrosse or soccer.

We started dating after college, when we were both living on the Upper East Side of Manhattan, starting our careers, living in shared apartments. I was working for my father's company, out of the New York sales office in Midtown, selling our manufacturing and distribution services to record labels up and down the Eastern Seaboard but mostly in the city. The compact disc had just been invented, and we were among the first companies making them, so business was good. Laurie worked on Wall Street, in a junior position at a big firm. The market wasn't great back then, in the early 90s, but she worked hard and did well. We both had money in our pockets, and we spent it all over the city together, falling in love over everything the big city of dreams had to offer: restaurants and theaters, dive bars and music venues, museums and shops.

Sometimes, on Saturday nights, when the weather was good, we'd stay till closing at a club or a bar Downtown, gorge on some Chinese at New York Noodle Town, which was open all night, and walk the whole way home to the Upper East Side as the sun came up and filtered mauve light down the side streets. We'd have coffee and warm bread, fresh from a bakery, along the East River with the sun fully up and the water placid and silver, and then we'd crawl into bed and sleep all day.

I guess that was our season for falling in love, but I like to think it began, at least on my end, with those car rides to and from Connecticut. And it occurred to me, in the back of a car, a taxi actually, on the way to the 40th birthday dinner with Mike and his date that maybe this was our season for falling out of love. Laurie was pissed at me, and I was pissed at her. We were late, and we were late because the babysitter she insisted on hiring was late; some kid right out of an art college in North Carolina, who was in the city trying to make it as an actress. She got screwed up on the trains trying to find our place in Brooklyn from the neighborhood where she lived in no-man's-land on the other side of the borough. I was happy to have Tina downstairs look after Josie when we went out, like she'd been doing since we bought into the brownstone she and her husband had converted into condominiums four years before.

Before that, after we got married, Laurie and I had moved around Manhattan, apartment to apartment like single couples do, but when Laurie got pregnant, we headed for Brooklyn before the wave of gentrification arrived because, being from Queens, I wasn't afraid of Brooklyn. We bought our first place in what realtors called a "diverse" neighborhood but was really a historical African-American neighborhood of various classes with beautiful homes. I loved it there, and I even made a good friend in a neighbor named Bill, a jazz and blues drummer who lived down the street. He wasn't as close to me as Mike, but he was the first close friend I had made as an adult, and a man I liked as much as any other, except Mike, of course.

Bill and I played tennis together almost every week, weather permitting, and he'd come down for dinner often or to sit on our front steps and drink beers with me in the late afternoon. Bill was the first person to hold Josie once we brought her home from the hospital, and the friend who saw her the most over her first five years of life. It was in that fifth year, though, that we said goodbye to Bill and our "diverse" neighborhood as Josie was about to begin kindergarten and the local public school wasn't so good; I had just quit my job to pursue my dream of being a writer and teacher, so private school wasn't an option, and Laurie insisted that we move. That's how we ended up as neighbors and partners with Tina and her husband.

Tina was Sicilian, and she says she sold us one of the units at a discount because she wanted kids in the building, a family to live upstairs. That was fine with me. Josie was five years old at the time, and neither my parents nor Laurie's provided much help. My father had sold his share in the manufacturing company and moved to Naples, Florida, with my mother. Laurie's family wasn't too far from the city but too busy with the bar to be doting grandparents. I understood. This was the world we lived in with families all spread out or too busy with life to help each other out. Tina was fairly young but old-school in that way. She didn't have grandchildren of her own yet, and her two grown sons were still enjoying their bachelor days in the city, so she latched onto us like we were blood.

Tina and her husband lived on the garden level with their own entrance, and the other three units of the brownstone were accessed through the front door up a set of stairs. We were on the 2nd floor up from the lobby, in one of the floor-through apartments, in between respective yuppie couples who lived above and below us. They were all nice enough, but younger than us, in their late 20s and childless, which made all the difference in the world with regard to friendship or things like that—and with their relationship with Tina. "You two go out," Tina would say. "I'll watch the baby."

But Laurie, for whatever reason, eventually had enough of the free babysitting and decided that this night of all nights would be the one to break from Tina and hire a sitter. We didn't know any sitters around because I'd take Josie to school each morning and pick her up after I taught English classes at a community college in downtown Brooklyn. So Laurie asked a neighbor, who had a full-time babysitter trying to make it in the city as a dancer. She wasn't available but her roommate, the undiscovered actress, could make it.

She made it, yeah, but 45 minutes late, and she showed up smelling like cigarettes, so even though she was late, she had time to catch a smoke before coming to our house to look after our six-year-old daughter. I didn't mention the smoke to Laurie in the cab as we fought about our lateness because I like an occasional smoke, too, and even had a soft pack of Marlboro Lights in the pocket of my sports coat for a few sticks after what I assumed would be one of the best meals of my life, but Laurie, after all those years working in the bar, hated cigarettes, and it didn't feel fair to go there. So I sat and seethed and looked out one window, while Laurie sat and seethed and looked out the other.

I occasionally, by instinct, eventually took a few looks at her tan, fit legs, exposed up to the thighs where the hem of her sleeveless, black Ann Taylor dress shimmied with each bump of the cab as it cut across 59th Street toward Columbus Circle. She always looked like a million bucks, as my father would say. My mother called her "stunning" the first time they met, and proclaimed that we were "made for each other." I thought that was funny because it was based on what? Looks? I dunno. But I thought at the time it was a mother's intuition at play and wanted to believe it. I wasn't so sure anymore about my mother's intuition because it wasn't just this night and being late for dinner that had us at odds.

We hadn't been getting along so hot ever since the baby was born. There were all these arguments, from the get-go, about who gets up more in the middle of the night and who changes more diapers and who puts her to bed more often. It felt like a competition, like Laurie's competitive instincts that she once accessed for athletics were finding its way into her parenting. It was always her coming at me with these things. And she wasn't always wrong; in fact, she was usually right, but why fight about it? And it got worse when she went back to work, and things hit the fan when I quit my job and went to graduate school. This was one of the reasons I didn't put up much of a fight about moving. I had spent my juice on the graduate school thing, and that decision was seriously in question, at least from one of us.

· ·

After my father sold his share of the compact disc manufacturing company, things changed for me a lot at work. The new management team was all over the sales department about numbers and expenses. They wanted me to go back and renegotiate some of my biggest contracts, to actually raise prices on companies we'd been working with for years. Yeah. Like someone can go in and raise prices on a company that has the choice to do business with anyone they want. At this point, compact discs had become a commodity, and there was a hell of a lot more available supply than demand. We were holding on for our dear lives. Prices were plummeting. Companies were getting discs made in China and shipped to the US for less than what we charged domestically. My father saw all this coming, and he also saw the threat the new technology posed with regard to simply downloading music instead of buying a whole album on a compact disc in a jewel box at 20 bucks a pop.

I was more concerned about not how the music was actually delivered but the music itself. I watched record companies change how they went about developing talent. The way they would, historically, sign bands and nurture them and give them a shot over the course of a few albums to find their sound, to find success. But as corporations went from not only distributing the physical products but to also owning the record companies outright, there was no more of this. It was all about profits, the fiduciary responsibility to make money every quarter, so for new bands, it was one and done if the debut album didn't sell. No more artist development. No more artists, really.

I admire musicians as artists. My father worked in the music business his entire adult life. Before going into the manufacturing side, he worked for record companies back when the people in the companies knew about music and cared about music. He brought home albums by the crate full and I'd sit in our basement with the headphones on, listening for hours and hours and reading the liner notes and the lyrics. The gift for playing music was not in me, but this made me love music and respect musicians all the more. The thing was, though, all of that reading of the lyrics taught me about storytelling and phrasing, which got me interested in writing when I was in high school. I used to joke that I didn't read books; I read records. I majored in English at college and dreamed of being a storyteller of some sort after graduating.

I went to work for my father instead. The music industry, back then at least, was known for nepotism. My father had a job waiting for me the week after I graduated college. Salary. Benefits. Clients. Expense account. Quarterly commissions based on performance. I didn't find this offer all that sexy or anything, but "storyteller of some sort" wasn't actually something I could apply for or expect to provide a decent living. I would need to go back to school to pursue writing for real, and I didn't want to go back to school at the time, so I took the job with my father's company. And it went well. I'm good with people, and I work hard. I love music. Sure, the job had its headaches and moments of absurdity and moments of complete boredom, but—for the most part—it was a solid job that paid well, utilized my skills for communications and relationship building, and had me eating in some exclusive restaurants and going to shows, not just in NYC but also throughout America via travel to cities like New Orleans, Nashville and LA.

But I saw the problems coming for the industry right about the same time my dissatisfaction with the job itself started to become an issue. My dad had already left the company, along with a couple of his cronies. Working for the company didn't feel right anymore. It seemed to me like a sign to make a change, to take a chance. I was in my early 30s, still somewhat young and optimistic but not stupid. Laurie made good money. We owned property in Brooklyn that was increasing in value like crazy. Josie was a toddler. A friend from college, and fellow English major, told me about this degree: Master of Fine Arts in Creative Writing. An MFA. I'd never heard of it, but he said it was a terminal degree and with it you could teach writing at colleges while pursuing your own writing. A college professor? And a writer? I liked the sound of that.

Laurie wasn't so crazy about the idea, but the fact that I would go to school at night and take care of Josie during the day appealed to her, mostly because we could let go of the seasoned nanny who Laurie thought took a little too much ownership over our kid. The nanny was always calling Laurie at work and screaming into the phone: *Josie did this for me; Josie did that for me.* It drove Laurie crazy. This was funny because Laurie didn't want to be a full-time mother, but she didn't want anyone else to spend so much precious time with her child either. I guess I was the least-worst option, so I applied to graduate school, got accepted at some super-liberal university in the heart of Greenwich Village and became a stay-at-home dad for a couple of years.

I did my best at caregiving and did a pretty good job. Under my primary care, Josie was well-fed and safe and, most importantly, loved. My favorite moments were when we'd lie on the couch after coming home from the park or some other excursion outdoors, and, after her lunch, I'd read a story to her with her body curled up against my side. I'd feel her drift off to sleep against my chest, and then I'd close my eyes and sleep a little too, her breath—in and out against my body—felt like we were floating in a sea of love. Looking back, I wouldn't change it for anything since Josie and I will always have that time, and that time—I believe—helped us form a bond that kept her close to me not too many years later when my life went off the rails, a process that began the very next day after our big birthday dinner at Per Se.

• • •

By the time we exited the cab at Columbus Circle and entered the shiny monstrosity of the Time Warner Center, catty-corner to Central Park's southwest corner, we were 25 minutes late for our 6:00 reservation. The sun was still out in early summer, and sweat moistened the collar of my dress shirt and started to gather under my arms. I had removed my sports jacket in the warm cab, but it hadn't helped much because of the tension. The fresh air outside felt good, though, and the brisk air conditioning in the spacious lobby offered some reprieve. We rode the elevator in silence and exited on the appropriate floor. I already had a sense of foreboding as this experience felt like high-end shopping in a luxury mall more than a fine dining destination. The incongruity smacked me between the eyes when we entered the austere waiting area of the restaurant and found Mike spilling out of an antique chair, holding a goblet of red wine.

"Whatcha drinking, Big Guy?" I asked.

Mike sniffed and said, "I think she called it a Barolo or something."

Oh, Christ, I thought. *We should have gone to Arthur Avenue in the Bronx or Peter Luger's in Brooklyn.* My apprehension faded, though, when Mike stood, tall and broad, fair-haired and bright-eyed, and opened his arms and flashed his million-dollar smile at Laurie. She melted and walked up to Mike for his massive hug, engulfing her in arms that threatened the shoulder seams of his blue blazer. Laurie loved Mike, and his presence always calmed her and made her, I believe, feel better about me. When Mike let Laurie go, he came for me. I held up my fist to pop it in his palm, but he brushed that gesture off and took me off the ground with a squeeze behind my back that popped vertebrae in my spine.

"Happy Birthday, And," he said, after putting me down, our eyes level but our shoulders two jacket sizes distinct. He leaned intimately close to my face and asked in one of his cartoon voices: "Excited for our birthday party?"

I smiled wide and tried to equal his enthusiasm for our little party, which struck me as smaller than expected as Laurie, Mike, and I made an incongruous threesome in the waiting area. A mannequin-like hostess stared at us, holding menus, waiting for our signal that it was time to be seated. "What?" I asked Mike. "Your date smarten up at the last minute?"

"Funny, And," he said, looking over my shoulder. "Here she comes."

A slender woman, with highlighted hair and wearing a slinky green dress, approached in heels and a practiced gait, one that makes it look like the legs are crossing over each other below shifting hips. She was pretty, of course, and younger than us, of course. I assumed Mike met her at the gym, where he spent most of his free hours when not at the fire station or behind the bar at a steakhouse in the West Village.

Her name was Danielle, and she was predictably appealing in many ways, though I assumed that she and Mike would date a few times and then remain friends. When it came to romance, Mike shied away from long-term relationships and resigned himself to the life of an active bachelor and serial dater with steady companions. This seemed to suit him fine, and he never expressed any desire to settle down or any skepticism toward those who did.

I understood why Mike didn't need to marry and have a family. He had grown into this figure that belonged to so many, almost like a public entity. His childhood was complicated by his years of not knowing he had a severe learning disability; those were the years when his persona was formed. He endured with dignity, ignoring slights and avoiding acting out. He didn't bully or take out his frustrations in any negative way. In fact, he took the opposite route and became this heroic figure of sorts, always looking out for people, making everyone feel included. It was like he covered up any insecurity he might have felt through an overwhelming display of confidence and genuine good will. He had empathy, writ large.

And because of this, Mike was the most popular person I had ever known. Everybody loved him: girls and boys, older and younger, parents, grandparents, teachers, coaches, priests. Even the nuns at Mike's Catholic school took a liking to him, and that was saying something because they were legendary for their cruelty toward little boys; Mike was the only kid around who went to St. Catherine's and didn't come home on occasion, if not on a regular basis, with knuckles lashed raw by rulers wielded by pious old ladies in habits.

Mike was the life of every party he attended, even if he showed up hardly knowing a soul. He'd just start talking to people, laughing it up. He made people feel good about themselves, where they were in that moment. If the biggest, toughest guy in the room was also the nicest guy in the room, then, well, how could you not have fun? It was some sight, this monster (Mike had grown huge in high school and stayed that way through early adulthood and middle age from hours and hours at the gym) working the room like it was his job. He was this combination of good cop, friendly bartender, big man on campus, boy next door, heartthrob; everybody's best friend. Mike had that classic quality of being someone that the boys wanted to hang out with and the girls wanted to date. And he did not disappoint.

My favorite thing about Mike in a crowd was how he'd instinctively find people who were not included or comfortable. Even as kids this was his thing. Some kid in the schoolyard sucked at sports, Mike picked him first and gave him a pep talk, smacked him on the shoulder, called him "Killer" or "Champ." Some kid's got holes in his shoes, Mike pays him a compliment of some sort. He did this subtly, obvious to no one but me because I was the most common witness to these acts of emotional benevolence. And it was as if he generated so much love among the people he encountered in his everyday life that he didn't need to start a family of his own.

He also had his own family, his parents before they passed and his four brothers and sisters, not to mention flocks of Irish extended clan, broods of McGoverns and Sullivans and O'Connors, who were big and close when we were young, and bigger and closer when we got older, providing Mike with nieces and nephews and cousins galore, all of whom he adored and spoke of constantly, boring the shit out of me with anecdotes of their accomplishments.

And, of course, Mike's perpetual single status left plenty of time for dalliances with the likes of Danielle in the slinky green dress, who had finished her prosecco and was smiling as Mike refilled her glass from the bottle he plucked from a bucket of ice. We were at a round table in the middle of the room and the sun was coming fuzzy through the windows as the sun went down behind the skyline and Central Park shimmered in a gauzy light specific to the end of cloudless days in early summer. I was starting to relax and feel better about this evening.

"And. And," Mike said to me once he finished filling Danielle's glass. "Tell Dani here about what your grandmother used to call me."

"Do I have to?" I asked, knowing that he was going to ask for this story and that I would have to tell it. And that no matter how many times I'd told it, and acted like I was annoyed at having to have to tell it that many times, I loved this story as much as Mike did.

"No. You don't have to," Mike said as if he had said the opposite and turned to Laurie. "Have you heard this one?"

"Once or twice," Laurie said, sipping prosecco with a bemused wink on her lips.

If only she were still as good-natured like that with me, I thought, before turning to Danielle in storytelling mode. "So, Mike and I grew up together," I started.

"He told me," Danielle said with a warm smile that warmed my heart.

"Right around the corner from each other," I continued. "So we saw each other practically every day."

"I know," Danielle purred, putting her hand on Mike's. "I think that's so cute."

So did I, but I pretended like it was no big deal and kept on with the story. "So, all the kids around, at least all the Italian kids, were always arguing about whose mother or grandmother made the best sauce, which really meant who made the best food overall. It wasn't a real argument, for the most part, because, of course, everyone always insisted that their mother or grandmother made the best sauce."

"Makes sense," Danielle said with a cute shrug. I was starting to like her. I stole a glance at Laurie, and she was either faking it like a champion or actually paying attention. I appreciated it either way.

"But the difference was that among our group of friends, I had Mike, and everyone knew that Mike, even as an Irish, loved eating more than all of us combined, so whenever we were having this argument, I'd turn to Mike and ask him: 'Who makes the best sauce around?' and the guys would all throw their hands up because they knew the answer."

I impersonated the guys by throwing my hands up and my head back and making a smirk. Danielle smiled widely, and Mike's face flushed a little red as he crossed his arms over his barrel chest. I gestured my hands toward Mike as if waiting on his answer.

Mike put his hands out in the familiar Italian gesture of certainty. "Nonna Mac," he said. "No doubt about it."

"My mother's family's name is Maccarone," I explained to Danielle, "so everyone called my grandmother Mrs. Mac, but Mike called her Nonna, the only person besides me and my family she allowed to call her that because she loved him so much and loved to feed him so much."

"Tell her what she called me," Mike said, leaning forward after signaling the sommelier with a spinning finger for more prosecco.

"I was getting there," I said, playing straight man to Mike's eager sidekick. "My grandmother called him 'Pasta Mike' because he would eat so much of her pasta. I swear, she'd make him a pound at a time, and this was before she covered it with sauce, you know, with cuts of meat and sausages and whatnot."

"Oh my God," Danielle gushed. "Pasta Mike. That is so adorable!"

"I guess, yeah," I feigned a half-hearted agreement, and then shared my favorite part of the story. "She'd always say to me, when I got home from somewhere when I wasn't with Mike, 'Your friend, Pasta Mike, stop by, looking for you' which was funny because Mike knew damn well when I wasn't home. I'd see him on my way out, and he'd ask where I was going. I'd tell him baseball practice or whatever. He'd say 'OK' and then go knock on our door."

Mike let out his big rip of a laugh and smacked the table, and his reaction was always my favorite part of telling that story.

· · ·

More prosecco came and we drank it down with the first of our courses in the tasting menu. It was some minuscule portion of hearts of palm salad, right out of a parody. Watching Mike's face as the mechanical-friendly server explained the offering was classic. He tried to look serious, as if he were paying attention, but I could see the quivering below his surface, as if he were dying to say something or just burst out laughing. Just as the server finished and left us to our tiny portions, Mike gusted laughter out of his nose and turned away to hide his buoyant face.

"You get that, Big Guy?" I asked him.

"Sure did," he said leaning with exaggeration over the table toward me. "Hearts of palm. Looks good."

"Don't eat it all in one bite," I suggested.

"OK, And," Mike said. "I'll try."

The alcohol made me feel better; it removed my anxiety and guilt. Laurie and Danielle were getting along nicely, and I started to think that watching Mike navigate the tasting menu might just be worth the price of admission. I could tell we would leave with moments to recall for a long time. "Remember the time when we were at Per Se..."

We went for the wine pairings with each course, just for simplicity, really, and they did a nice job with that. The food improved with each course, as well, and there were some moments of exaltation, though watching Mike's face as each plate was explained outshined anything they could do with food. And we had fun along the way.

After Mike gobbled down a piece of toasted brioche slathered in foie gras, he turned to Laurie, who was cleansing her palate with a crisp Côtes de Gascogne and had yet to touch her plate. "You gonna finish that?" Mike asked her.

Laurie laughed out loud and heads around the room turned in our direction. "You can have mine,"

Danielle said earnestly to Mike, with her hands on the sides of her tiny plate.

"I was just kidding around," Mike said to her with a look of affection and then a quick look at her plate.

Danielle was a personal trainer from Staten Island who was studying to be a nurse. She and Mike had not met at the gym, as I suspected, but at the steakhouse where Mike tended bar. She was on a first date with a stock broker Mike described as a "stiff," who spent more time on the phone than engaging his date during their pre-meal cocktails. "I felt bad," Mike said. "Poor thing had no one to talk to."

Danielle laughed and waved Mike off with the playful sarcasm his sense of humor warranted. A joke between me and Laurie was her commenting on one of Mike's many companions, whether she liked her or didn't like her, and me saying definitively, "You're never going to see her again." That's just the way it was, but I was thinking, high above Central Park, in the shiny auspices of that swanky restaurant, that Mike had brought Danielle for a reason and that we might actually see her again. The idea of Mike finally settling down occurred to me as our final savory course was explained.

We had a choice of loin of lamb or Wagyu beef. They didn't serve Wagyu beef yet at the old-school steakhouse where Mike worked, so he asked for an explanation. Our mechanical-friendly server explained that Wagyu beef is from specially raised cows in Japan that are regularly massaged by human hands. She also mentioned for the second time that this choice came with a hefty supplemental upcharge. Mike ordered the beef.

"For that price," I said to Mike after the server left. "You should be the one getting rubbed by Japanese hands."

Mike howled his big laugh and smacked the table. The room went silent for a second. "Good one, And," he said after the room's din returned. "Good one."

Dessert was forgettable and the check was staggering. Mike tried to pick it up, but I insisted on going halfsies like always. My head spun from the moment I registered the amount owed to offering my credit card to signing the bill. Next thing I knew we were out in Columbus Circle, the traffic whizzing by and night breezes lifting the hems of the ladies' dresses. Mike had a hot dog in each hand, and I smoked a cigarette as tourists and night-goers flitted past. The mood had shifted, and I fought a feeling of sickness and regret. My much-anticipated after-dinner smoke tasted like shit.

"Let it go, And," Mike said between bites of his dirty water dogs piled with sauerkraut and onions. "Let it go."

I studied the treetops in Central Park, which swayed gently. Mike polished off his hot dogs and took Laurie's elbow in his hand. "You should have never let this guy go into teaching and writing," he said, seeking levity through humor, but Laurie wasn't having it.

"I don't remember being asked," she said.

That crack from Laurie about "not being asked" put an end to the night. Mike knew that Laurie and I had a beef over my new vocations, and he felt bad about making a joke that gave Laurie an opening to stick it to me. We said our goodbyes, and Mike and Danielle went home to probably tear each other's clothes off, and Laurie and I rode home in silence with no sex planned for our immediate future.

"Go for a drink?" I asked when we got out of the cab in front of our building.

"Nah," she said. "You go."

I went to a bar around the corner that was set up to look like an old social club, with its attempted implications and hints of membership. The bartenders had waxed mustaches, suspenders, and shirt sleeves rolled and clipped tight around their elbows; they shook classic cocktails and served them in champagne glasses. Sepia pictures of gangsters were on the wall. These hipster attempts at ethnic credibility cracked me up. There was even a group of hipsters around the neighborhood who got the key to the long-dormant bocce courts in the neighborhood park and started a league.

The faux social club bar was the closest one to home, and it was fairly empty on a summer night, with most of the neighborhood newbies gone for the weekend, so I got a spot at the bar and sipped whiskey they made in nearby Red Hook that cost as much as if they brought it over from Ireland one glass at a time. After a couple of cost-prohibitive after-dinner drinks, I walked around the neighborhood until I assumed Laurie was asleep.

I crept inside the building and into the apartment. Our bedroom faced the street, and Josie's room was in the back. I tiptoed into her room and could see her face clearly in the moonlight that slanted through her window, and the silhouettes of her stuffed animals all around the room. She was asleep sideways with her back to the wall, so I took off my shoes and lay down on my back, above the sheets, next to her. I figured I'd stay for just a minute, enjoying the rhythm of her heart beating through the mattress and her sweet breath in my ear.

I woke in the morning with Josie, bug-eyed, kneeling over me with her face a few inches from mine. Her chestnut hair was in a ponytail and she stared at me with adorable yet baffled, dark eyes. "Whatcha doing, Daddy?" she asked in her sweet, singsong way with just a hint of suspicion.

"Nothing," I said. "What's going on, kiddo?"

"Nothing," she said. "Wanna play *wiff* me?"

Before I could answer, she had me by the hand, pulling me out of her room toward her basket of dolls kept in the living room. We plopped on the floor. She dug in the basket for a couple of Polly Pocket figures.

"You be this one," she said, handing me the figure known as Drew as she clutched Polly in her other precious hand. "And I'll be this one."

And so began the torture and humiliation of parenting when somewhat hungover. I'd avoided such situations for the most part, but I also wasn't entirely unfamiliar with the exercise. Polly Pockets were among the worst to handle when addled in any way since they were tiny figures subject to costume changes of itty-bitty, rubbery outfits and accessories. I thought my head was going to explode getting Drew out of his top and into a sleeveless vest (the look I always gave him).

"You OK, Daddy?" Josie asked.

"Yeah, fine," I said. "Why do you ask?"

"You smell funny."

"Oh, sorry," I said and felt like a failure. "I've got an idea."

"What?"

"Let's get breakfast sandwiches and eat them in the park."

"But it's Saturday," she said. "Aren't we going to have spaghetti pie?"

Spaghetti pie was Josie's favorite breakfast. It was basically a pasta frittata, made by mixing leftover pasta with a lot of whipped eggs and grated cheese, and then baking until solid. I loved it, too, and we had it most Saturday mornings after our Friday pasta nights, but there was no pasta the night before, so there was no spaghetti pie in the morning.

"Sorry, kiddo," I said. "Pasta Mike ate all the pasta at the restaurant, so no spaghetti pie."

"Oh," Josie said. "OK."

"But we can have breakfast sandwiches instead," I suggested. "Come on."

"OK, Daddy," she said. "Let's go."

. . .

There's no real cure for a hangover, as far as I know, but bacon, egg and cheese on a roll from a New York deli — along with some strong coffee and fresh air on a summer morning — certainly works better than sitting on the floor changing pliable outfits on tiny figures. Josie picked apart her sandwich and gave me the rest before running off to chase pigeons. I was enjoying the reprieve before what would surely be at least an hour on the swings when my cell phone buzzed in my pocket. The screen displayed "Mikey." I thought he was calling to brag about his night with Danielle. I was already smiling before I spoke. "Please spare me the details, would ya, pal?" I begged.

"It's not that, And," Mike said, his voice heavy and even flecked with gravel. "It's not that."

I could feel the bottom falling out. It was a single sentence, vague at best, but something told me that something was terribly wrong, that the world was about to change in an instant. "What?" I asked. "What is it?"

"I think I'm sick," he said.

"It's called a hangover, Mike," I said, grasping onto any thread of hope I could find. "You should get a load of mine."

"It's not a hangover," he said.

There was noise around him, beeping and voices.

"Where are you?" I asked.

"New York Presbyterian," he said.

"The fuck for?"

"It's my chest. My lungs," he said. "They think it's got something to do with 9/11."

. . .

When I speak of Mike in terms of heroism, I'm usually doing so with regard to all of the other days of his life, other than 9/11, because all those other days demonstrated characteristics, albeit often quiet ones, that defined his heroism in my eyes. I was especially impressed by Mike's capacity for love, how the whole of his heart could take in so many. For that, he was my hero. For most everybody else, though, Mike became a hero on 9/11.

I had been in our Midtown offices that morning when the first plane hit the North Tower. It was only a quarter to nine or so, and I was alone in the office because record industry people didn't start early, but I liked to get into the office and handle paperwork and such before the phones started ringing. I'd heard the sound of the first plane crashing into the building. The boom was not that uncommon in New York, and I thought it was a truck hitting an especially big pothole. Seriously. A little while later, I went to the coffee shop downstairs where everyone had their eyes glued to the TV above the counter. Everyone: cooks, waiters, manager, patrons. It didn't look that bad from the angle, and not too long before that day some imbecile recreational pilot had flown into one of the Towers, so I was thinking that it had happened again. I got a large coffee to go and was almost out the door when a second boom, much louder, came from the south. The people in the coffee shop screamed, and everything sort of went still for a moment. And then everything went nuts.

Terrorism. Terrorism. Terrorism. People were beside themselves with fear and outrage. The city was under attack. The city was under attack. Sirens suddenly came from every direction. The coffee shop filled with people who stared at the TV. I went outside and stood on the corner of 44th and Lexington. It was such a beautiful day.

It seemed like all the sirens in all of the city were blaring toward Downtown. People ran past on their way Uptown, frantic like in a disaster movie, away from the sight of the smoke that billowed darkness into the perfect sky beyond the corridors of Manhattan avenues. More people flocked past on their way Uptown. Some were on their phones, frantically dialing or yelling. I had a cell phone then, my first. The thing was about the size of a shoe, and I pulled it from my pocket and looked at it. And then I thought of Mike. He had called my cell phone the night before. He was at the supermarket with a bunch of firefighters from his ladder company in Hell's Kitchen. One of them had a phone, and he had borrowed it to ask me what he needed to make meat sauce for pasta. I told him. He thanked me and said his shift would be over the next day and that he'd be in touch about getting together.

I started running Downtown, against the flow of pedestrians and vehicles. At first, I didn't know why, but I figured out it was the sirens and what they portended—not because there was a massive catastrophe in motion, but because my oldest friend was surely riding on one of the trucks making all the noise, heading straight into the heart of chaos. The giant phone rumbled in my pocket, and I stopped to answer it, thinking maybe it was Mike again, having borrowed a phone to call me like he had the night before. My breath came in and out ragged, as I was winded and freaked out.

"Oh my God," Laurie asked. "Are you OK? Where are you?"

"I'm fine," I said. "I'm on my way Downtown."

"Are you fucking nuts?" she screamed more than asked. "Do you know what's going on?"

Actually, I didn't know what was going on. All I knew was panic in the people and mayhem in the streets. The Twin Towers were on fire and, I assumed, Mike was on his way to put it out. Laurie had been at a doctor's appointment back in Brooklyn that morning, which was why I wasn't worried about her. And she was working at home those days anyway, for a firm out of Stamford, Connecticut, so there was no connection in my mind whatsoever between her and lower Manhattan. At least, that's what I told myself as to why I wasn't thinking of her on the most tragic morning in all of our lives.

She told me what was going on—planes had been hijacked by terrorists from the Middle East, and that there were other planes missing, too, maybe more coming for New York. Lower Manhattan was a shit show, and that I needed to get home to Brooklyn. She had just got back from the doctor: She was pregnant. "Come home," she said. "Now."

• • •

It was an awful day to find out you're soon to be a mother or a father, though I kept thinking of all those people who were actually having babies that day, and how their children's birthdays, the infamous day they entered this world, would always be associated with death and destruction. And, of course, the overwhelming feeling was for all those people who were losing their babies and loved ones that day.

My stomach churned and my head spun as I walked home thinking about Mike. It wasn't like I wasn't excited about becoming a father. We'd been trying to get pregnant for six months or so, and there was an exhilaration threading through me from the news, but it was just that: news. Abstract. It wasn't Josie, yet, or even a boy or girl for all I knew. What I did know was that the person who had been by my side my whole life was, at that moment, probably running into a towering inferno.

I adhered to Laurie's demand and fought the urge, as I walked down the east side of Manhattan, to go look for Mike, to tell him to "Come home. Now." Putrid smoke, a malevolent shade of the darkest gray, billowed, almost cruelly, it seemed, over the magnificent Manhattan harbor, below the pristine blue sky, toward the tree line and rooftops of Brooklyn. People hurried and stumbled and ambled in shock over Brooklyn Bridge. They resembled refugees in some faraway land, not Americans in our greatest city. I walked briskly, pushing past the slow footed or those who had stopped to turn and look at the unimaginable. I checked my phone again and again as I gained on the bridge's apex and descended into Brooklyn.

I walked over to Flatbush Avenue and through the housing projects on the lower reaches of our neighborhood. As I made my way to the Heights, folks were gathered outside, like a block party almost, comforting each other and talking over each other. People cried and yelled. Grown men freaked out. Jet fighters flew over, low and loud. When I finally turned the corner on our block, sweaty and dusted in soot, my heart beating and my breath short, Laurie stood up and reached out her arms although I was 50 yards away. She was with Bill, who also stood, a bottle of beer in one hand. The last lengths of the walk home felt like as long as it took to make it that far, from Midtown Manhattan to Clinton Hill, Brooklyn. Bill came into the yard with a cold beer extended.

"How ya doing, buddy?" he said, the most compassionate smile on his face.

I took the beer and made the only face I could muster, a mix of relief, befuddlement and anguish, and trudged up the steps into Laurie's arms.

"And it looks like your buddy is OK, too," Bill said after I settled into the warmth of Laurie's embrace.

"What?" I asked, pulling back from Laurie and looking to her for an answer.

Laurie began to cry and smile. "He's OK," she said. "He's OK."

"Who?" I asked. "Mike? Mike's OK?"

"Yeah," she said. "He was just on TV. He was carrying a woman out of the buildings, over his shoulder. It was in the background, behind a reporter, but that was definitely him."

I felt born again.

• • •

When I walked into Mike's hospital room at New York Presbyterian, he was upright on his bed in a medical johnny gown, tubes hooked to one arm and monitors attached to his chest. "And," he said and held out his palm. "What's going on?"

I couldn't speak, so I just smacked my fist into his hand and touched his massive shoulder. One of Mike's older brothers was in the room, talking fast into a cell phone. All of his siblings were super successful, and this one, Rob, was a Wall Street guy who retired in his 30s and then went back to work for kicks and charity. He acknowledged my presence with a half-smile and went back to his conversation that seemed to involve Mike and logistics.

"What the fuck?" I asked.

"Taking some tests," Mike said with a smirk. "Find out the deal."

"Deal with what?" I asked. "How bad could it be? You were fine last night."

"I wasn't fine last night," Mike said.

"Could have fooled me."

"It's been bad for a while."

"For how long?"

"I dunno," Mike said, turning his head toward the windows full of muted light. "A few months. Maybe longer."

Mike's brother clamped his phone closed and started talking in a very officious way to Mike. He had made arrangements for Mike to go to another New York hospital, one with a unit that specializes in lung disorders. "Best in the city," he said, before correcting himself. "No. Best in the country."

"OK," Mike said. "When we going?"

"Now," his brother said and walked out the door to make the arrangements.

Mike and I looked at each other for a few seconds. "Can I come?" I asked.

"I don't think so, And," he said. "I don't think so."

• • •

I walked out of the sterile, crisp hospital lobby into a harsh curtain of New York summer air. The hospital was way Uptown and a long way from Brooklyn. Occasional breezes off the river provided some relief, but I was sweating through the back of the short-sleeved dress shirt I changed into after hurrying Josie home, waking Laurie up and explaining what was happening and where I was going.

After a quick cleanup, an "Italian shower" as Mike would call it, I hustled to the subway and made it to New York Presbyterian, with slow weekend subway service, in 90 minutes. It didn't occur to me to take a cab, I guess because I'm a New Yorker and was working on instinct. Taking a cab back was not of interest, as getting home didn't have much appeal. I was lost in New York, my hometown.

I walked one hundred blocks south to the 59th Street station, turning my head regularly to the north, toward Queens, looking for a ballast in a city I'd lived my whole life but now felt foreign. I had stripped down to my sleeveless T and felt like a throwback to the 50s as I tried to find ways to avoid the new reality that was as serious and undeniable as the high summer sun over Manhattan that slapped my bare shoulders and anguished head.

Deep down, I had feared something like this. Mike, in many ways, seemed invincible to me, but there were lots of reports about the damage done to the lungs of anyone who was anywhere near the Twin Towers that day and the days and weeks after, especially firefighters. Mike was not only among the first responders, he spent the next few weeks down there on the pile, digging through the wreckage and trying to clear the blight on our beloved city.

His heroism that day, captured on the often-repeated footage, was widely known, and it made Mike a legend in a city looking for people to lionize.

Mike had no problem with the attention at first, but he was smart to stay off the news programs and talk shows that sought his appearance. His public fame faded, though he remained in the favor of a lot of power brokers, one of whom treated Mike and a couple of his ladder mates to an all-expense-paid trip to a private resort in the Dominican Republic that was so exclusive I couldn't find it on the internet.

The gig tending bar at the West Village steakhouse also came as a result of Mike's new status. People wanted a piece of him, a symbol of courage in the face of danger and a source of balm to a scared city. Mike had worked the bar at the gin joint in our old neighborhood, Brady's Irish Haven, pouring pints and brown liquor for measly tips from the old-timers who drank the daylights out of perfectly fine afternoons in the dreary space along with a nicked bar and faded photographs, a stench of soaked floors and defeated men. The place was always happier, festive even, when Mike was behind the bar, a towel over his shoulder and validation for those who had their drinks poured by the neighborhood kid who had done good and still stuck around.

· · ·

I'd moved out of the neighborhood as soon as I graduated college and only popped in on occasion to Brady's when visiting my parents. Once they moved to Florida, I never stopped by the bar, but I was happy about the steakhouse gig after 9/11 because it coincided somewhat with my big change, quitting my job and going to graduate school for creative writing. The university was near the steakhouse. Classes met two nights a week, and I'd go by afterward on nights Mike was working. He'd give me free drinks and dinner of a steak or a chop or seafood at a place that catered to Wall Street types with expense accounts or more money than they knew what to do with. So, yeah, the high-end meal and top-shelf liquor was appreciated, but it was Mike's company that got me through.

I was insecure about my graduate school program. The professors were successful authors; my fellow students were all better educated than I was, or—at least—much better read and knowledgeable about literature. Their vocabularies spun my head, as did their familiarity with literary devices and classic works. They were, for the most part, also younger than me and in New York from prestigious undergraduate programs on their way to being the next generation of major American writers. I was a kid from Queens who read liner notes growing up and liked to tell stories.

Still, I held my own in the program, mostly because I knew how to tell a story while most of my elite classmates were figuring that part out. I got along fine within the program, too, but my classmates and professors were not my friends. We were cut from a different cloth. Most in the program, including the instructors, would go after class to a university hangout around the corner, a bistro with black and white photos of musicians and authors and artists. Dim lights. A long bar. Booths in the back. They'd ask me to join, but I'd pass and go see Mike to drink and eat for free at a well-lit steakhouse and launder my insecurities in the juvenile bond shared with my oldest friend.

"Mikey," I'd prompt after settling into the bar and numbing my lips on an ice-cold martini Mike had just shaken the shit out of, and then ask him questions about things I'd heard that night but knew little of, but knew Mike had no clue either and could share in my ignorance:

"You ever feel like an unreliable narrator?" – *Sometimes...*

"When's the last time you came across a MacGuffin?" – *The breakfast sandwich?*

"What's your favorite line from Beowulf? – *The End*.

"Ever read any Balzac?" – *You're making that up.*

My favorite, though, was when I asked him if he knew about a "distinction without a difference" — which was something one of my classmates had commented on in workshop that night about a scenario in my novel. "Got me there, And," he said and walked away.

A little while later, when I was polishing off a NY strip with some fries, Mike sauntered over and put his hands on the bar in front of me. "I think I got it," he said.

"Got what?"

"A distinction without a difference."

I could tell by the smirk forming at his mouth and the insouciance in his eyes that the response was going to be raunchy. He leaned forward so as not to be heard by anyone but me. "A distinction without a difference is when, maybe, you're banged up in a bar or something and you go home with some girl you don't know, and maybe, with the lights out, you can't remember what she looks like, but what's the difference?"

Mike smacked the bar and stood up, his arms over his barrel chest.

"Thanks, Professor," I said. "I appreciate the clarification."

"Anytime," he said and walked down the bar to fill an order at the waitress station.

• • •

Mike, thanks to his brother's influence, had been transferred to a hospital associated with New York University. It was Downtown and much easier for me to reach, though going there was not easy at all. I'd hop on the subway between classes and pop in for 15 minutes or so and then hurry back to campus and then home to meet Josie in the playground when school let out. All the running around was easy compared to what it was like to be there with Mike.

Seeing him in the hospital was excruciating. Someone that vital did not belong in such a place. He didn't fit in the bed. The hospital gowns didn't fit him. The doctors and nurses were topnotch, but there was not much they could do. The damage to Mike's lungs was epic, and he had waited way too long to report any problems. I didn't think of his reluctance to report his pain as some sort of tough guy code or anything; I figured Mike didn't want to cause people to worry, so he hoped upon hope that the pain he experienced would just go away.

I knew how he felt. Every time I walked in that room or called Mike on the phone, or even when my phone rang, I had this hope, tucked like a feather in the cap of my heart, that there would be a miracle reported. I'd never heard of Joan Didion before graduate school, but she was apparently a god to the well-read crowd. We read some of her essays in a class dedicated to literature, and I quickly recognized that she had great style and a way with insight that I admired. I'd even read, on my own, her memoir about loss, *The Year of Magical Thinking*, and I knew exactly how she felt during those times of staggering uncertainty. I wish I didn't know how she felt once the real hurt arrived.

The failure of a miracle to arrive crushed me on a regular basis. The weight of it stayed with me, and I could sense myself changing. I was aware of my becoming less in many ways. There was less joy, which was obvious, but there was also less presence in both a literal and figurative sense. I was often late getting back to work and even missed a few classes. My department chair was a friend and knew what was going on in my life, but his patience began to run out. I had become that unreliable narrator occasionally found in novels. But mostly, it was the figurative absence that defined me. Just a lack of focus on the world around me. Maybe I used all of my goodwill and life force trying to project positivity upon Mike as I sat with him in those stolen minutes during my weekdays or for longer periods on weekends. Moments that left me drained and eager for them to end. I hated visiting Mike, but I also felt a need to do it. He had plenty of visitors, pals from the FDNY and friends from growing up. His siblings were there all the time. Old girlfriends appeared regularly. He didn't need me there, but I went anyway, even though it made me disappear.

"What's wrong, Daddy?" Josie would often ask me, every time as if it were the first time.

"Nothing, kiddo," I'd lie, though I knew she began not to believe me.

This subtle disconnect from Josie was the first portentous inkling of a truism that was coming my way: When you fall out of love with life, people fall out of love with you.

• • •

Mike died on the second day of January. The end came on fast, and I was still living in denial, doing my best Joan Didion "magical thinking" when I got a voice message from Mike's brother, Rob. "I'm sorry to have to tell you this, Andy," his heartbroken, recorded voice informed me. "But Mike's not going to make it. If you want to come to the hospital to say your goodbyes, you might want to do that right away."

The last part, about saying my goodbyes, I didn't really hear at first because I collapsed on the kitchen floor when I heard "Mike's not going to make it." I must have screamed or moaned or something because Laurie and Josie came running from the bedroom in the front of our apartment.

"What happened?" Laurie asked.

"Daddy! Daddy! What's the matter?" Josie wanted to know after she joined me on the floor.

I remember being in a sort of upright fetal position against the cupboards and breathing very hard in and out of my nose. My stomach hurt, like I'd been shot with a cannonball at close range. I don't know how long I was like that, but I snapped out of it when the anguish on Josie's face and in her voice finally registered with me. "I'm sorry," I said, sitting up with my back to the cupboards and Josie now tucked tight at my side. "I'm sorry, but it's Pasta Mike."

"Pasta Mike!" she squealed. "What happened to Pasta Mike?"

I felt so ashamed for not having told her already about Mike. She loved him, and he loved her more. I had a picture on my desk of her as a toddler in his arms, asleep on his chest on the couch in our old place. The look on his face is of such joy, such profound contentment that I'm at a loss to describe it. I can only assume that he felt a part of Josie because she was a part of me, and that our forged lineage connected them. I used to take solace in knowing that Mike would always keep Josie safe, that nothing could happen to her while he was around.

I didn't have the heart before to tell Josie that Mike was sick, and I definitely didn't have the heart now to tell her that he would soon die. I kissed her forehead and got us both to our feet. I'd become a coward in the face of all this, and Laurie looked at me with pity as she took Josie away by the hand. "Come on, sweetheart," she said. "Let's go to your room and have a talk. OK?"

Josie questioned me with her eyes as she walked out of the kitchen, holding her mother's hand. I sensed some possible betrayal in her look, along with concern, but I had no ability to empathize effectively in the moment. I put on my coat and shoes, grabbed my things and hustled down the stairs, out of the building, across the courtyard and onto the sidewalk. I moved quickly but everything felt like slow motion. It was a weekend morning in winter. Hardly anyone was around, and I felt like the only person in the whole world.

I waited on the corner for a cab. The wind delivered cold air, and I recall wishing I'd worn a hat because my ears stung and my nose hurt. The taxi reeked of pine-scented air freshener, and the driver tried to chat me up in broken English before he got the gist that I didn't want to talk. I thought about, on the way into the city, how Mike used to love to talk to cab drivers. He'd sit up front, even if there was room in the back, and just pepper the drivers with questions about where they were from and, if they were immigrants, how they liked America, and what they did back home before coming to our shores to drive a cab. "What, are you writing his life story?" I'd ask sarcastically from the backseat after Mike's probing went on too long, and he would shoot me a look like I had two heads and go back to his conversation with the cab driver.

• • •

I got out of the cab in front of the hospital. There was commotion out front, and I thought of how irrelevant time was to emergencies. There were no morning emergencies or evening emergencies. They were all the same, and time meant nothing to their realities. That's how I felt walking in the hospital that winter morning. It could have been the middle of the night on the 4th of July, and the circumstances would be no different. Time stood still; time didn't matter. Nothing mattered other than the reality I was about to face.

Inside the hospital, on Mike's floor, a group of his family were in a special waiting area. I guessed this was the pen for those who were there to say goodbye. The room had no windows and dark paneling. Durable chairs. A silenced TV fastened in an upper corner. A lot of faces that resembled Mike's gathered, varying in ages and genders. Some spouses added a different dimension to the fair-haired, bright-eyed Irish brood who dominated the room. Mike's brother, Rob, reminded some of the nieces, nephews, and older siblings who I was, "You remember Andy Cotto, right? Mike's friend."

It felt nice to be referred to as "Mike's friend" and I could tell by the way many in the room looked up when overhearing my name that they knew who I was. I knew who they were, even those I hadn't seen in years or even ever met, because Mike talked about them all the time. They got together a lot, never in the old neighborhood, though, but at one of their big houses in the suburbs or spacious apartments in the city. According to Mike, every one of his siblings and every one of his nieces and nephews were superstars, the absolute best at whatever it was they did. Ride horses or play golf, do financial planning or clean teeth. They were all the ultimate in Mike's eyes. Masters of the universe. And he had a point, but still, my eyes would roll back in my head when Mike began to tee-up some tale about one of his family members, "And. And," he'd say, "You know my nephew, Sean..."

"Christ," I'd mutter and play along. "What about him?"

And Mike would just go on and on about something Sean or whomever he brought up had accomplished. And there was no face of stultification I could make, no number of finger-pistols stuck in my mouth, no feigned yawn so stifling, that could get him to veer away from the enthusiasm and pride of the storytelling or the length. "How about a Cliffs Notes version?" I'd sometimes suggest after he broached one of his relatives in the familiar manner, but he'd just continue on as if I hadn't said a word.

Brother Rob led me from the room of Mike's family that functioned as his muse, and I thought, while walking toward the isolated area where Mike lay dying, of all the little things I'd miss about him, even stories that really had no relevance to me beyond the storyteller himself and his enormous capacity for love. I wondered, for the first time, what he used to tell his family members about me. I knew he was proud of me for becoming a writer. He used to tell everybody. When I was at the bar, he'd say to one of the regulars or someone on staff I hadn't met, "This is my oldest friend, Andy Cotto. We grew up together our whole lives. Tremendous author, this guy. You should read his book."

My first book sold to a small publisher shortly after I finished the Master's program. It was the coming-of-age story about a kid from Queens. One of my favorite memories of Mike was him at my book release party. We had it in a music venue, to be different, more festive than most book events. A band played; the bar was open; there were food trucks outside. Mike got there early in a sleeveless argyle sweater that I used to bust his chops about because it was simply too much pattern for a guy his size. He looked like a preppy sailboat, but he loved to wear the sweater just for the looks and especially the ones I'd give him. The look that defined him that night, though, was pride. He made himself into the unofficial host and worked the room like he owned it, which he did. He bought all the signed copies on display that he could carry and handed them out randomly. The sight of him with all the books in his arms, scanning the room for potential recipients, is one I'll always treasure. And I'd remember that look every time I had doubts about my choice to pursue writing.

The hospital room that held Mike in his last moments smelled funny. Medicinal and stale. Eerie light slanted through the drawn shades. We might as well have been on Mars, as far removed from normality as it seemed. Machines, beeping and registering, filled most of the floor space, except for the bed that held Mike. His torso was elevated, and his shaved head thrown back to one side; his eyes were closed and his mouth wide open, taking tortured breaths.

I'd never seen anything so horrific. I thought of that painting by Edvard Munch. Then I thought of putting a pillow over my oldest friend's face, to end his suffering. And that was the thing, in that moment, at least: not the dying, but the suffering. I'd never seen Mike distressed by his own pain, not even the time when we were little and he fell off the monkey bars and broke his arm in two places, but now the ultimate agony reverberated out of him like the tortured gasps coming from his mouth. I'd never prayed before, but I prayed to God that my friend was not afraid.

I tried to say something; that's why I was there, after all, to say my goodbyes. But my jaw quivered when I opened my mouth to utter the word "Goodbye." I wondered if he could feel me; if he knew I was there. I stood in silence as long as I could, hoping that he was still alive enough to sense my presence and hoping that having me in the room brought him some comfort. Words were not an option. Clichés or confessions had no currency. Nothing mattered. The friend I had known and loved my entire life was no more. He was dead. Mike O'Shea was gone.

Brother Rob cleared his throat from the threshold. Some relatives were behind him, holding their coats and looking forlorn, waiting for a turn to say goodbye to Mike. I looked at Mike one last time and walked out the door, down the hallway and past the waiting area. I did not stop. I held my fist against my nose and over my face as the elevator dropped toward the lobby. I thought I might faint or spontaneously combust from overwhelming emotion. I can't recall wanting anything more than for that elevator to reach the ground floor and for the doors to open. I beelined through the foyer. The frigid air punched my nose and slashed my already watering eyes after I pushed through the revolving door. I cut hard right and tucked into the concrete columns beside the glass facade where I cried as hard as I'd ever cried in all of my life, and knew — beneath the blubber and release — I was entering the world of suffering and loss.

• • •

Some random stranger had handed me a fistful of tissues, and I thanked whoever it was without turning my head away from the corner of concrete and glass in which I was buried. When the tears stopped, I cleaned up my snot and salt-streaked face, bunched the remaining tissues in my coat pocket, and then I lurched off in search of the nearest bar.

The first open drinking establishment I passed was a cheery Irish place on the corner of an east side avenue. They had just opened, and the only other people at the bar, at the elbow by the door, were a couple of Irish maids who had stopped for tea on their way home from the market. I slipped past their carts piled with groceries and sat at the far end of the long bar tinted the color of redwood. The walls were bright red, and I imagined this was intended to keep the place bright, but the radiant motif made me think of hell.

The bartender had a ruddy, stoic face and coarse, gray hair Brylcreemed along the sides and flipped back up on top. He had the air of the bar owner and recognized someone there on business as opposed to pleasure. "Can I get ya?" he asked.

"Vodka, rocks," I said.

I sat slumped, my shoulders lifted up toward my ears, as if a clothes hanger was still in my shirt, my eyes on the bar, sipping steadily until I had enough vodkas to lift my head and remove myself from the rabbit hole I'd scampered down. I'd had four glasses of straight fire on an empty stomach, and I looked around the barroom for signs of life. Muted light swarmed the front windows, reminding me of visions of entering heaven like they did in movies.

The old ladies down the bar had been replaced by two younger guys in hoodies, one on either end of the elbow, money and cigarettes on the bar in front of them, talking over each other in Gaelic accents. A soccer game was on the TV, and it had their attention. I smelled French fries and meat coming off a grill.

The seasoned bartender brought me a menu, but I held up a hand and ordered a cheeseburger, medium-rare, without considering the options. "Very good then," he said and walked away. I could sense his relief at not having to pour any more booze into a sad sack on a fledgling Saturday afternoon, but I wasn't done drinking. I put a coaster over my beveled liquor glass and went outside for fresh air.

When I got back, the cheeseburger was on the bar in front of my spot. I ordered a Smithwick's on my way to the bathroom to pee and wash my hands. I dried my hands on a fresh bar towel beside the sink and looked at myself in the mirror. My eyes were red, and my pallor was sickly from drinking despite the invigorating cold that still clung to my skin. I splashed water on my face and rubbed my eyes. I blew my nose in a paper towel and took a deep breath. The thought flashed through my head that I should leave, to take the burger to go and to go home. I entertained this thought, and even believed it had been accepted, until I resumed my seat at the bar and took my first sip of what would be many beers and my continued introduction to the insidious melody of alcohol and grief.

• • •

The abundant winter sunlight, angled and sharp, made it hard to see when I walked out of the bar, though it felt good to be outside after so many hours in the muted, stale barroom. The afternoon had warmed up slightly, and I could feel the vitamins of the sun absorb into my skin as my pupils struggled to adjust to the new surroundings. I was drunk in the middle of the afternoon, numb more than wasted as I nursed my last few beers and took lots of water on the side. The bartender nodded and said "Aye," when I asked for the check.

I wanted to go home, but I didn't want to go home, either. The latter wasn't an option anyway as showing up in this condition would not go over well, nor would it be appropriate, so I called Laurie and lied through measured words intended to hide my debilitated state: I was having a late lunch with Mike's siblings and I'd be home before dinner. She said, "OK" and encouraged me to be careful.

The cold began to pinch my ears, and my nose stung from the wisps of wind that appeared from the west at every intersection. On St. Mark's Place, I went into a gift shop and bought a thick, wool FDNY hat and pulled it down over my ears as I returned to the streets, mostly empty on a cold, midwinter Saturday. The East Village denizens, those who were out or were without homes to be within, barely registered to me beyond vague figures and tufts of breath. My habits of sensory observation, my bread and butter as a writer in my opinion, had been suspended, and I drifted slowly down 2nd Avenue, as if on a slow, moving sidewalk in the airport.

I crossed into the Lower East Side as a sense of sobriety threaded into my consciousness. There was nothing to do, not eat, drink, nor anything else available in the most vibrant city in the world, paralyzed emotionally and spiritually as I was, so I trudged closer and closer to home in what felt like a death march, the cold creeping into my bones with its sights on my soul. The plan was to walk the Manhattan Bridge and take Court Street all the way to Carroll Gardens, sobering up enough before reaching home and avoiding, as I walked, thoughts about what the next days and weeks would involve.

• • •

Over one thousand people showed up for Mike's wake. It was held at the funeral home in our old neighborhood, and the line from the opening hour till closing went around the block. I went alone and was one of the first to enter. Pictures from Mike's life were displayed through a corridor that led to the place in the chapel where Mike's body awaited visitors in an open casket. The pictures mostly featured Mike's family, formal portraits from various years far into the past, with Mike, the youngest, gaining on them all in size with each passing year. There were school portraits and class photos. Most of the others featured Mike in adult life, again, mostly with his family, but now at social occasions, weddings and holidays and birthday parties.

We didn't grow up in a time or place where parents took tons of pictures of their kids with other kids, so I wasn't surprised by the absence of still-life shots from our childhood. The only picture I had of us was one tucked in my wallet that I had found in my parents' house when they were packing up to move to Florida. It had been on a collage, sealed in shellac, taken by my father when Mike and I were about eight. We were both in hand-me-down baseball uniforms, our arms around each other's shoulders, Mike's posture ramrod straight, me with a hand on a hip pivoted to one side. That pose was familiar to our childhoods, as it was how we often walked around, arms thrown casually around each other's shoulders without hesitation.

The photo gallery made me smile, and I understood why this was customary for wakes, which functioned somewhat as celebrations. I dreaded the funeral, but the wake promised to be a reprieve of sorts, and a chance to honor Mike in a way I imagined he would appreciate. My mood elevated even more when, after a collection of FDNY photos, I came across a small exhibit dedicated to me and Mike. The photos, which must have been found among Mike's belongings, featured us two together in an array of venues, from my wedding, to us on vacations together, to us at parties. It's funny, in every one (except the one of me struggling to hold up Mike across my arms in a hotel pool in the Bahamas) we have our arms around each other's shoulders.

I skipped paying my last respects to Mike in his open casket. I made some shit up in my head about having seen him already in practically the same state, and that there were other people waiting. The truth was that I was feeling some relief for the first time since my battle with suffering began, a relief not brought on by the consumption of medicinal martinis, as I described them and prescribed them each night, but just by a general sense of collective love for Mike that informed the room. Mike's family was, of course, front and center, all dressed up and shiny and displaying great dignity, even elegance somehow at such an awful occasion. The FDNY was in full effect, too, from the bagpipers outside to the legions of men in uniform huddled in traffic-inducing circles. More than a few men in brass had lingered and even stood with the family at the front of the chapel.

I gravitated toward a group of kids from the neighborhood, some who had come from out of state to pay their respects. We had fun catching up, and I appreciated how they paid their respects to me, as well, as if I were standing next to the casket with Mike's family and brass from the FDNY. The kids from the neighborhood knew, better than anyone aside from Mike's family, the special relationship we had, and I felt validated, in a weird but comforting way, by their focus on me. They all seemed excited about the Irish wake to be held afterward at Brady's. I was looking forward to that, too, especially since I had a fun story to tell about an impromptu trip to Ireland that Mike and I had made in what would be among the most memorable days in a lifetime of friendship.

• • •

The bar filled to capacity and then overflowed soon after the wake ended. I'd gotten there early, cutting out of the funeral home with a few neighborhood kids. We sat at the far end of the bar in the dingy room, sipping beers with the locals until the respective crowds from Mike's wide-cast life began to fill the space. The cold snap persisted, so the removal and storage of winter weather paraphernalia contributed to the fast-filling room. The owners soon removed a panel that functioned as the back wall most days, except for certain events, that doubled the floor space, but that was soon cramped, too.

Someone yelled, "Call the fire department! We're violating capacity!" Laughter erupted throughout the room, but the capacity issues had me concerned since it fostered my sense of anonymity among the sea of faces, but it also complicated my chances of telling a story I'd been rehearsing in my head for days.

One of the rank and file firemen hopped on a bar stool and began the festivities by declaring the Irish part of the wake officially in progress and that anyone who had a story to tell about Mike could do so by raising their hand and being granted the floor. A few dozen hands went up, and the room began to stink of congestion and spilled beer. I turned from my spot at the far end of the bar, and began to make my way toward the back in search of fresh air until a hand gently patted my shoulder. "Look, Andy," Mike's brother Rob said, so close I could smell the gum on his breath. "My family and I are heading home, as we have a huge day tomorrow and this looks like it might go on for a while, but I want you to know that we have a space for you to speak tomorrow at the reception after the funeral. OK?"

He looked hard into my eyes and held them. "Thanks," I said. "I appreciate that."

"Of course," he said. "You are Mike's oldest friend. We all know that."

"Thanks," I said again as brother Rob turned and shouldered his way patiently through the crowd.

The relief washed over me as I went the other way, through the throng of mostly strangers, toward the back to get some fresh air on the makeshift patio the owner had built a few years prior to accommodate the no-smoking ban inside New York City bars and restaurants. Some of the guys from the neighborhood were out there with a cache of warm beer cans and a bottle of whiskey lifted from a supply room. "And what do we have here?" I asked in my best brogue.

They laughed, and I was handed a can of beer and a shot of whiskey. And then I told them, under the light from a single exposed bulb, a group of men my age standing around or sitting on crates who had grown up with me and Mike, the story of the time Mike and I were in Italy for our 30th birthdays and how we ended up in Ireland for a day, after Mike had heard, from a college girl studying abroad and sharing a table with us at a Florentine trattoria, that flights to Ireland were fast and cheap. I told them how Mike insisted that we leave right away to find his relatives in County Cork, and I talked him into leaving the next day; how we went to the airport first thing the next morning and bought two round-trip tickets on Ryanair to Cork Airport and back to Florence that same night; how Mike insisted that I drive the rental car since his dyslexia would surely put us into a tree considering the complications of vehicles and traffic directions in the UK, though I knew he just wanted to drink all day, which he did, starting in the airport in Cork and along the way in every colorful village we passed on our way down the coast to the town of Skibbereen from where his family hailed. All Mike knew about his possibly living ancestors, besides their hometown, was the name he had heard once from his mother, of a bachelor named Timothy O'Shea who lived outside of town on a small farm and rode a bicycle into town each day, rain or shine, for supplies and a pint of stout.

"You're kidding me, right?" I asked Mike after his initial inquiry, directed at a puzzled barmaid at the first pub we stopped at within the proximity of Skibbereen. "That's all you got?"

Mike shot me his familiar look of bemused annoyance, sipped his stout and studied the room for another person to ask. "You should work for one of those ancestry companies," I said to him.

"Good one, And," he said. "Good one."

Later in the day, after unsuccessfully storming Skibbereen, and 10 pints of Murphy's Stout and counting for Mike, we stumbled upon an ancient man in sagging, threadbare wool clothes, taking some sun on a bench outside a storefront. I begged Mike to leave what I believed to be a sleeping man alone, but Mike got his attention and asked him if he knew of the relative in question. "I believe I just might," the man said, suddenly alert. "Have you a vehicle?"

Mike was so excited, and he led the frail man by the arm to our car. I followed the man's directions out of town and along otherwise abandoned lanes carved into dense woods. Mike sat in the back with the man who stared out the window when not turning his head toward the front to tell me where to go. Mike sat up and looked like a four year old on his way to a favorite destination. "You sure about this?" I asked the man when we'd clearly made a concentric circle and were surely on a road already twice traveled.

"Course I'm sure," he snapped, his wan face shading toward ruddy.

I caught Mike's eye in the rearview and registered my skepticism. "Just keep driving, And," he said.

We eventually entered an unmarked two-way of dirt that snaked along a craggy coastline of a murky inlet bordered by rocks. "There," the man said, pointing toward a listing saltbox with a pitched roof in back and a neon Murphy's sign in the front window.

"Is this a pub or a house?" I asked the old man.

"It is but one and the same," he said with a chuckle as I pulled the car down a driveway covered in mussel shells.

Mike smiled and anticipation filled his face. "Does my relative live here or drink here?" Mike asked.

"Who?" the old man asked, as he exited the car and made for the front door.

"Let's get out of here," I said to Mike. "This guy's senile or crazy or both."

"No, no, And," he said. "He's legit. I can tell."

"You can tell?"

Mike took a big breath through his nose. "I can tell," he said and got out of the car and followed the path the man had taken inside. I decided to just wait in the car until the charade became obvious to Mike, tired of this half-assed pursuit, but after 20 minutes of waiting, I crossed the yard and entered the front door with a small "Open" sign on display. Mike sat on a Naugahyde couch in an ancient living room, his vibrance in contrast to the muted tone that cloaked everything else, including two elderly women who sat in opposite corners in rocking chairs; one knitting, the other working on a crossword puzzle. Mike, a pint of stout on his thigh, widened his eyes when I entered.

"And, And," he said. "Get a load of this. These two sisters…"

"And those that came before us," one of the sisters, without lifting her head from her stitching, interrupted Mike for clarification purposes.

"And those that came before them," Mike recognized, "have run this bar out of their home here for over 100 years. A hundred years. You believe that?"

"Wow," I said, noting the musky smell of beer absorbed by carpet. The room was a typical living area from a previous generation, except for the bar that ran along a side wall, with a single tap for beer. The shelves behind the bar held dry goods in boxes alongside jars and cans of preserved foods. Some household items were off to the side, stacked on a separate shelf. I wondered how long the products had been there and when the last time was that they had made a sale.

"Grab a pint, And," Mike said. "I'm running a tab."

The glasses were lined on the bar, and I took the cleanest looking one and held it under the tap as the dark, effervescent stout roiled out and foamed as it filled the glass. I sat next to Mike on the couch, and he smiled at me like he used to when he was a child, and it occurred to me that Mike was still a child, and that was one of his best qualities.

I sipped my stout and looked around, determined to see this through with my friend. "So where's our guy?" I asked optimistically.

One of the sisters turned her head away from me to hide her smile. I looked at Mike. "He's in back," Mike said, his head turned from me, too.

"Doing what?" I asked.

"I dunno," Mike said, chin now on chest. "Might be taking a nap."

"Might be?" I asked, losing my short-lived reverence for my friend's childish ways.

"No 'might be' — he's fast asleep," one of the sisters said. "There's no doubt about that."

I looked at Mike with exasperation. He held up a hand in assurance and then got up to help himself to another pint. He sat down next to me, and we sat in silence for another half hour, interrupted only by Mike entering my peripheral vision every few minutes to make sure I registered his mirth. Finally, the man came out from the back area, stretching his arms overhead and recalibrating his afternoon. Mike stood to greet him. The man looked startled. "And who are you?" he asked.

"I'm Mike O'Shea from America," he said, desperation entering his voice. "You were helping me find my relative, Timothy O'Shea."

The man rubbed his chin and squinted at Mike. "Let me ask you something," he said.

"Sure," Mike said. "Ask me anything."

"Have we had this conversation before?"

Mike's face went flat as I got up from the couch to put my pint glass on the bar. "You and me?" Mike asked, devoid of disbelief. "We had this conversation earlier today."

The man rubbed his chin and did his best to recognize Mike. The sisters went about their business as if nothing unusual transpired in their living room/commissary/bar. "Let's go, Mike," I said, and walked out the door.

Mike joined me in the car a few minutes later, looking dejected and fatigued from disappointment accompanied by too many pints. "Don't even say it, And," he said, fastening his seat belt.

I gave my friend some berth and focused on getting out of the area, which wasn't so hard since we'd traveled the same roads numerous times on the way out there. When it was clear I had found the route back to town, which would take us to the highway north to the airport, I looked at Mike. He looked at me. "Let me ask you something," I said, impersonating our elderly Irish friend. "Have we had this conversation before?"

We both cracked up and laughed about our absurd adventure over the course of a day in Ireland during our holiday in Italy celebrating 30 years of friendship. And we kept talking about that day in the subsequent years with, "Let me ask you something," making it into the vernacular we alone shared.

When telling the neighborhood guys the story in our own private wake, I left out much of the flowery prose and extraneous details, but that's the version of the story I always kept in my head. We sat around out back for a while more, collectively sharing stories from our childhood, not all centered on Mike but mostly so. By the time we exhausted our canon of adolescent recollection, the wake was finishing up and the bar emptied. I was pretty drunk, and it was pretty late. It would be hard to find a cab around there at that hour, and I didn't want to take the subway from Queens to Brooklyn in the middle of the night, so I called Laurie and told her—focused on sounding sober, once again—that I was going to sleep at my parents' old house, in the empty apartment upstairs from the main level we rented to a lovely family of Dominican descent. The key was with the others on my key ring, and I knew the apartment upstairs, not occupied since my grandmother died, was in good shape as I'd been by recently to oversee some work being done on the roof. What I didn't know was that my anticipated one-night visit to the apartment would not be an aberration.

• • •

Laurie came over with the car the next morning. She brought me clean undergarments and a fresh suit to wear to the funeral. Josie was in Long Island with her grandparents, and Laurie looked great in a sleek black, long-sleeved dress and pearls around her neck. Her coat, the brown suede one with fur cuffs and collar that I had brought her back from Italy, was draped across her lap as she sat on the edge of the couch in the front room of the four room apartment, the parlor area that faced the street, while I showered and shaved and tried to let the water refresh my numb senses. The old TV in the parlor and the transistor radio in the kitchen were off, and the space remained silent as I got dressed, burdened by a sense of dread.

I refused breakfast or even coffee, just making sure to drink lots of water to remain hydrated after a long night of drinking. I'd gotten used to the fatigue from drinking, of feeling sick and tired, and functioning under such conditions, though I recognized that patience was a certain casualty in the war with alcohol and grief.

"You all right?" Laurie asked me as I expressed some frustration with the traffic on the local street that would take us to the Brooklyn Queens Expressway. I insisted on driving, just to keep my mind occupied on something, though I regretted it as soon as I was reminded of the aggravation of driving anywhere in New York City on a weekday morning.

"I'm fine," I answered without diverting my eyes from the traffic ahead of us.

"You out late?" she asked, with an uptick of tension in her tone.

"Not really," I said.

"It was pretty late when you called," she countered.

"Give me a fucking break, would ya?" I barked and turned to her as I said it.

Laurie lurched her shoulders, but not because of my words but because of what I didn't see. "Look out!" she yelled.

I slammed the breaks and stopped just short of the car in front of us that waited at a traffic light. It felt like lava rising in my esophagus with the fumes trying to escape my ears and from behind my eyes. "Maybe I should drive?" Laurie suggested kindly.

"It's OK," I said, feeling like an asshole. "I got it."

The funeral ceremony was at a church on the outskirts of Queens, in a suburban setting near the border with Nassau County. The church was large and fairly modern, of brick facade with white columns and trim, on a spacious piece of land with a great lawn in front and a parking lot in back that was already half-filled when we arrived. We parked and crossed through the cold air under a sheet of ice blue sky. The familiar sound of bagpipes accompanied us as Laurie put her hand inside my arm in what I deemed not so much an act of intimacy but of guidance. It felt like autopilot until we found our way inside the church and into the pew where we would sit, without removing our coats, for the next 90 minutes, though it could have been a minute or a lifetime.

The formality of the fire department and their solemnity defined much of the proceedings, as men in dark uniforms, heads down, faces furrowed, dominated the space, along with Mike's large and extended family who filled the first rows of pews in their shining Irish beauty. The pallbearers were a mix of FDNY and a few of Mike's nephews. At one point, during a sonorous sermon by a Catholic priest who didn't recognize the magnitude of Mike's death, it occurred to me that I might be having an out-of-body experience, somehow removed from the confines of my physicality into a surrealism that existed in another realm. This was when, out of nowhere, my heart began to wallop inside my chest and my throat clenched. I couldn't breathe. My head felt light, and I thought I was going to fall over or disappear. We were in the middle of the row, still in our coats, with people pressed tightly on either side. I closed my eyes and focused on breathing through my nose as sweat moistened my shirt.

When I opened my eyes, brother Rob was delivering a eulogy that captured Mike's spirit and uplifted the room, inspiring laughter and tears. Laurie held my hand and gave me a wan smile. "You OK?" she mouthed. I nodded and paid attention to the words about Mike, and then I remembered the words I had prepared for the post-burial reception. I figured Rob would be on the tribute, the standard speech of praise and accounting of the accomplishments and humanity of the deceased. My idea was to have some fun in recognizing the things that Mike loved, from the mundane to the profound, though my speech would have to wait for another time.

• • •

We trudged out of the church through another assault of bleating bagpipes. The sound captured the anguish, and as much as I admired the pageantry and meaning of it, I wished they would please stop playing. The keening sound hurt my ears and pierced my heart. It reverberated on the waves of cold air and accompanied us across the lot without decreased volume. I couldn't wait to get away from the elegiac whine and shut the car door, start the engine and turn on the heat, to get away from the reminder of what it all meant.

We followed a procession of fire trucks, their lights flashing, leading an army of cars on a slow roll to the cemetery gates. The trees within the grounds were bare and the grounds, planted with mausoleums and gravestones, seemed to quiver with the approach of another soul. I thought of battlefields in the moments before fighting. I thought of the sensory torture all of this pageantry provided, and I felt ashamed for being so sensitive. "Come on, And," I could hear Mike repeat one of his father's generational mantras: "Grab a glove and get in the game."

I did my best. In a courtyard within the confines of the cemetery's administrative area, I shook some hands and hugged some distraught girls Mike and I had grown up with. And then I got in line and waited with what felt like thousands of others to give a final send-off to the closed casket that held Mike O'Shea. The day was clear and cold, though the scene felt gauzy to me, with wool coats and hats, scarves and gloves, plumes of breath rising like smoke from a chimney. The approach to the casket, elevated on a pedestal, went along quickly, with most simply touching the top of the polished, wooden box and moving on. There was, it appeared, no more time for weeping or reflection, just a quick "So long" seemed to be in order, and I felt relief that the end of this long goodbye drew closer with each shuffle forward. The actual burial was for the family only, and everyone else was invited to the country club in Nassau County for a lunch, followed by tributes from a few select speakers, including me.

My mind was on the speech, and I rehearsed it in my head as I trudged along the line. Suddenly, though, I was in front of a mahogany box of which my friend was inside. Where he would be, as the priest repeatedly said, "forever and ever." I'd watched people touch the box upon approach and quickly move on. I tried, but I couldn't. I lifted my hand, but my entire arm no longer felt like part of my body. I pictured Mike in that box and terror came over me. Either he was telling me something or, worse, he wasn't telling me anything at all. I grew terrified and confused. I didn't want my friend in that box. How could he be in that box? How could he be dead? The episode of panic that rattled me in the funeral service returned, and now that I had a physical choice to respond, as opposed to being stuck between mourners in the pew, I bolted. As fast as I could move, short of running, I crossed the courtyard and moved away from the administrative area and the cars and the people.

My breath heaved from my chest, and tears froze to my face as I marched across the access road and into the cemetery grounds, past skeletal trees, gravestones and mausoleums. It didn't feel real, but it hurt so bad. Competing with the overwhelming sadness was a sense of shame. So many people, especially Mike's family, behaved with such dignity through all of this, and here I was, a kid he grew up with, walking without direction through a cemetery, crying uncontrollably. Eventually, my senses began to return, and the clean, cold air cleared my head.

The access road curved around the grounds to the gates, and I set my eyes on that as a destination with a plan to walk the road back to the parking lot alongside the administrative area, but when I reached the gates, Laurie was there in our car. She had followed me from the casket and watched the direction I took across the grounds. I was cold and tired and very happy that she was waiting to help with my escape. I got in the car.

"What do you think?" she asked gently. "Go straight to the reception?"

The sleeve of my coat was smeared with the snot I had wiped repeatedly from my nose during my retreat through the cemetery. I looked in the mirror behind the sun visor: My eyes were blood-red, my hair a mess, my face and skin, unfamiliar. "Let's go home," I said.

"You sure?" Laurie asked. "What about your speech?"

"That's alright," I said. "Let's just go."

• • •

I called Mike's brother the next day to apologize for skipping the reception. He told me not to worry and that he understood. He said that we would be sure to stay in touch, that Mike would have wanted us to do so. We made some plans I figured would never happen, and said our goodbyes. His kindness was a relief, and I recognized that a reason Mike was such a good guy was that he came from such good people. The phone call with Mike's brother also felt like the end of something, like this torturous passage would now be over, but I was wrong about that.

I went back to work a few days later, at the start of a new semester, the spring semester, even though it was January, which wasn't lost on me from a symbolic standpoint. Spring was the season of new beginnings, and mine would surely arrive. The routine of being back to work provided some focus and relief. After dropping Josie off at school in the morning, I'd walk a mile to downtown Brooklyn, to the community college where I taught five sections of English Composition, two on Monday/

Wednesday and two on Tuesday/Thursday, with a single, elongated class on Friday morning. I loved teaching, and the community college population of diverse learners from typically underprivileged backgrounds matched my personality and faith in education's impact.

My first class on Monday through Thursday wasn't till late morning, so I'd go to the nearly empty Writing Center to work on a novel in progress, a noir set in Brooklyn on the dawn of gentrification, before I taught back-to-back classes at 11:30 and 1:00. After the last class, I'd take the same walk back to pick up Josie from school at 3:00 sharp.

After school we'd hang out in the schoolyard, weather permitting, or go home and find things to do in the apartment, either alone or with a school friend of Josie's. For me, though, the afternoon—no matter what we did—was about killing time before dinner. I always thought about dinner, looking forward to it all day, the last meal a highlight of my day, a regular occasion that involved planning (I'd stop on the way home from school for ingredients and wine), preparation (my mother and grandmother taught me how to cook, and it was one of my favorite hobbies), and eating with Josie and Laurie (on the nights the latter was home in time).

Laurie had returned to a Wall Street firm, and her hours were long. She'd get up with Josie in the morning, have her ready for school an hour early, before I woke up to feed her and drop her off across the street. A regular work day for Laurie was 8:00-6:00, and this did not make her happy as she felt like she was missing so much of Josie's life. I got this, but I didn't know what to do about it. Finance was her career of choice, and these types of hours came with the job. The fact that I had, essentially, the same hours as Josie was a silent source of tension. "That's great," Laurie would say when I shared a story of a particularly adventurous afternoon or even just one when we sat around watching TV.

The latest I could hold Josie off from eating was 6:00, so most nights I'd keep dinner for the adults warm on the stove or ready to be made when Laurie rolled in around 6:45, if we were lucky. I'd do my best to save a small dessert for Josie to have while Laurie had a glass of wine and I got our dinner ready. While Josie ate, I'd sit with her and have what was once a simple aperitif, a glass of wine or a prosecco, maybe a Campari spritz in summer. Nothing hard. But after Mike died, and I resumed what I assumed to be a new normal, "medicinal martinis" became part of my routine. And they weren't even martinis at all: no vermouth; no olive; just ice cold vodka in a classic martini glass that I'd put in the freezer before leaving for work in the morning.

The effect was immediate, a numbing of my lips with the first sip and a soothing of my frayed nerves as the depressant went down. It only took a few sips before my spirits improved, and I really could have done with half a glass only, but I could not convince myself to stop as the succor provided impaired my judgment. I'd time the drink to coincide with Laurie's return, and sometimes I'd slip a few extra splashes into the glass if time permitted (and I managed to make sure it did). I'd be good and cocked for dinner, though I'd hide it from my daughter, who didn't know what daddy was drinking, and my wife, who didn't know how much drinking I'd done.

By the time we'd finish a bottle of wine with dinner, I'd be drunk, though still functional. Laurie would take Josie in back to spend time together and then get ready for bed, and I'd do the dishes, careful not to break anything. And even though I'd stopped drinking after dinner, the alcohol still slithered through my veins and a restlessness permeated. One night Laurie came from the back, sized me up, and suggested I take a walk. So I did, after picking up a pack of smokes from the bodega on the corner. And this began my new routine of a walk after dinner, down to the Brooklyn waterfront in Red Hook, one smoke on the way and one smoke back. Two total. I told myself this was not abnormal, that people around the world spent their evenings this way, drinking and smoking, and, besides, my new bad habits were both temporary and necessary.

The routines, so to speak, both good (writing every day) or bad (getting shit-faced each night and taking cigarette walks) kept me occupied somewhat as each day became an exercise in avoidance. Memories of Mike interrupted me throughout the day, and especially when my guard was down during times of either not being immersed in creativity or succored by liquor. The experience was relentless as it was jarring, just a normal moment alone or in front of a class or talking to someone else, when a thought of Mike would arrive and ruin everything. I assumed this was a temporary condition, a phase of grief that I was entitled to because we had so many memories, and that, eventually, this "new normal" I kept hearing about from people who spoke of grief would arrive like a new day and the life I previously enjoyed would return, minus a key figure, of course, but livable nonetheless.

Spring weather arrived, and my boozy evenings continued as the smokes picked up to four a night, two each way to the waterfront and back. I wasn't particularly worried about the health ramifications as I was still fairly young and in good shape. I had added exercise to my regimen to battle the sluggishness in my body and fog in my brain, the latter affecting my ability to write. The exercise helped a lot, and also connected me in a positive way to Mike as he was a fitness fanatic.

I imagined Mike with me when exercising, hearing his encouragement as I pumped out push-ups and sit-ups from our bedroom floor in the morning when Laurie was getting Josie ready for school. On the weekends, with more time available, I'd do a workout Mike loved: The Murphy. This was a hybrid cardio/body effort named after a fallen war hero Mike worshiped, and I'd picture Mike with me as I ran to the calisthenics station in a park near the waterfront, where I'd do, without pause between sets, push-ups/pull-ups/air squats, until the requested number of each was met, and then I'd run home.

The clarity I felt after such exertion provided enormous relief. My head felt unburdened by spider webs, and my lungs took in and sent out the type of air that fuels the engine of our existence. I'd also experience brief bouts of optimism, a release from the steady gloom that surrounded me, and a sense of well-being at having spent some time with my friend. Mike often spoke of exercise being as much about mental health as physical, though I always thought that he was full of shit, justifying the amount of time he spent building his enormous body. Now I knew that he was sincere, and that he had given me a gift and a semblance of togetherness.

Even with the addition of regular exercise, and a positive connection to Mike, I was still a mess for the most part, though it probably wasn't obvious to most people. I did my job and met my responsibilities; I kept up appearances and stayed out of trouble or at least stayed in the shadows. Still, the suffering persisted, despite the respite from exercise, and a numbness began to come over me. I could feel a retreat from the light of life, though I denied this to myself and did my best to hide it from the people most important to me. Josie remained my angel and biggest fan, but Laurie wasn't so easily fooled.

"You all right?" she'd ask me on a regular basis, her tone threading genuine concern with hints of impatience. And she'd always ask just before leaving for work or a moment when there wasn't time to talk, as if she were just checking in. I really didn't blame her for any frustrations as it's hard to maintain such a relationship with someone who had changed for the worse, especially someone who didn't seem all that interested in dealing with their situation; someone who failed to realize that the problem was bigger than they were.

And that really was the problem, not so much the grief alone but my shame at being so waylaid by it. Mike was not my sibling or uncle or cousin. We did not have the same last name. We did not sleep in the same station house nights on end, or run into burning buildings together. We grew up together. That's it. Two kids from the same neighborhood. Sure, our friendship was special, but it was just a friendship. Mike's loss should have not had any practical impact on my day-to-day life, my ability to function as a husband and father, to make a living, to pursue my dreams. This failure of recognition and the inability, as a result, to deal with my grief was why I didn't talk to anyone about my situation and why, as a result, my problems persisted and eventually came crashing down.

• • •

One spring evening, on my way back from the waterfront, the breeze at my back and my buzz still intact, I remembered that my phone had vibrated in my pocket as I was chatting with Josie during her dinner and my medicinal martini. I always vowed not to be that parent who checked their phone in front of their children, despite the temptation that communication triggered, so I let it shimmy until it stopped. A few seconds later, another signal from my phone indicated a voicemail, which was somewhat unusual as I, at that point in my life, got few phone calls and even fewer voicemails, though the thought faded as my nightly routine proceeded as normal.

When I remembered the voicemail on my way from the waterfront, I pulled out the phone and stopped to sit on the steps of the majestic Catholic church a few blocks from home. The street was empty and quiet. A soft breeze conjured polite applause from the new leaves that quivered against each other. The moon covered everything in a veil of gentle light. A sense of optimism came over me, though I didn't know why until I accessed the voicemail, and the number indicated a 212 area code, which was Manhattan, a place where, at the time, I had no other connections except to the publishing industry.

It was an agent. A big one. She had read the excerpt of my noir and loved it. The authors to whom she compared both the story and the writing didn't seem real, those I could never have imagined being mentioned within the same sentence. "What?" I said out loud hysterically and lost track of the message. I replayed it to make sure I wasn't dreaming. I wasn't, and there was more: She wanted to read the rest of the story and requested an exclusive on the entire manuscript.

"Holy shit," I said to the sky. "Holy shit."

This was big. Really big, as an exclusive pretty much guarantees acceptance, especially since the rest of the novel was even better than what she'd already read. I put the phone carefully into my pocket so as not to damage the invaluable message it contained. I plopped my elbows on my knees and raked my hands through my hair, letting the spring air and the spring news surround my body and fill my lungs. The uncertainty of writing, of embarking on something so challenging with such limited chance of success, is far more debilitating emotionally than most people, even writers themselves, recognize. The amount of rejection that comes with the effort creates an insecurity and hurt that has to be, in some ways, ignored if one wants to persevere. I'd heard in graduate school that publishing is harder than writing, and I soon learned that to be true. I'd been lucky enough already to have a book published by a small press, but now I had taken a giant step into the big leagues with a big-time agent who praised my work in unimaginable ways and requested the rare exclusive.

The sense of validation filled me with wonder, as if I were a little kid and something magical had just occurred. A burden, like a phantasm, lifted from my body and drifted off into the Brooklyn night, leaving me feeling electric and alive. I quivered like the overhead leaves and jolted to my feet. I looked around and patted my pockets as if looking for someone or something. I couldn't figure out what my body was telling me to do until I felt the phone in my pocket and yanked it out. I instinctively thumbed through my contacts to find Mike's number. There it was, illuminated on my screen: Mikey.

The dropped phone cracked against the cement steps as I collapsed back down on my ass. I began to weep, slowly at first and then harder and harder, my hand over my mouth and hot tears pouring from my eyes. I cried and cried for how long I didn't know until I picked up my head and confessed to myself and the Brooklyn night, "I miss my friend."

The words sort of chugged out of my throat, so I said it again more audibly: "I miss my friend."

I felt so weak, like such a baby, but I knew what I said and what I felt were true: Mike's absence haunted me and would forevermore, or so it felt in that helpless moment when massive joy turned, in an instant, to unbearable pain. Was this the "new normal" I heard grief experts, both actual and amateur, talk about? Would every bit of good news, every special experience, get wrecked by the fact that it couldn't be shared with someone who ought to know? That can't be "normal." I wondered how I was going to live like this and then I dashed that morbid thought.

I picked up my shattered phone and slumped off the steps toward home. It wasn't too late, around 10:00. People slowly walked dogs or hurried home from the subway station. Sounds emanated from the windows of brownstones: music and television and conversation. I felt entirely alone and wished to be home, to transport myself immediately to our front garden, to be somewhat safe from suffering, but when I arrived at the gate, going inside didn't feel like an option. Josie was surely asleep, but I didn't want Laurie to see me like this. I latched the gate with a click and strode away from home.

I gravitated toward an emptier direction, down low-slung streets that led to the polluted canal of the industrial Brooklyn lowlands, lined with cement factories and scrapyards and abandoned lots. I crossed a gravel and weed-covered expanse and stood on the rotted railroad ties that buttressed the canal banks. The elevated train tracks and the darkened Kentile Floors sign were the only presence in the otherwise empty sky. No one was around, nothing except me and the lonely moon that hung overhead like a lost soul. I couldn't decide, as I stared at the light shimmering on the murky surface of the canal, if the moonlight intended to console or mock.

The water, only a few feet below, didn't move at all. I thought of the dead German Shepherd that Laurie and I once saw floating in these fetid waters, and a shock tore through my entire cavity. My feet and hands felt severed. I fought to keep my balance, before managing to stumble back and fall onto the gravel. I got to my feet quickly and scurried away, panting, as if being chased by the thought of death being better than this kind of life.

I tempered my pace closer to home, on a busy road that ran parallel to the elevated train tracks. I felt exposed, as if I'd done something that needed a cover-up, like a criminal escaping the scene of a crime. My nerves settled as I approached our corner, though there was no desire to return home, so I passed our block and popped into the local bar, the hipster joint, and kept my head low while surveying the dark room. Predictably, there were no parents out drinking at this hour on a school night, just a bartender in an antique dress shirt and the sound of a game of pool being played in back, so I settled into anonymity in a dark alcove by the front door with a beveled glass of amber liquor that comforted me like a thick shawl thrown over my pinched shoulders.

I slouched and sipped the whiskey, escaping with each swallow the harrowing thought that struck like lightning on the banks of the canal. Before that moment, the idea of actual suicide had never entered my mind in all of my life. It was an abstract concept, unfathomable, a great mystery never to be considered beyond the associated tragedy and sorrow and unknown origins. We— those of us not afflicted by such thoughts, probably as a means of rationalization and avoidance— considered those who took their own lives as "others" or maybe, being most reductive and ignorant, as perhaps "sick."

And I knew as I sat there alone in the dark alcove, candlelight flickering off yet another beveled glass of whiskey, that I was not suicidal, but I had been privy to its lure. I had felt the logic behind it. The temptation. Now I understood why people take their own lives: The suffering is so profound and so relentless, so seemingly insurmountable, that death must be more appealing than life, as death is the only way to stop the never-ending ache.

I shivered thinking of those poor souls, ones I now considered as far more sympathetic and immediate compatriots. A guttural chuckle escaped my dry throat, and a complicated, layered illumination mushroomed in my understanding of life. It was as empowering as it was scary, yet something like redemption wiggled through the morass of emotions and enlightenment knowing that I, like characters in stories who are blessed by being witness to another reality, had seen the darkness before being engulfed by it. I heard Mike say in the back of my head, "At least you got that going for you, And," as I approached the bar and ordered another drink, already thinking about the next.

. . .

I woke up on the couch, upright, fully dressed, except for my shoes that were sprawled across the floor. A cascade of water soaked the side of my head and spread down my shoulders and side. I hopped to my feet and felt the ground shake. "What the fuck?" I asked Laurie, who stood behind the kitchen counter that bordered the living room, holding the spray faucet extended from the sink. She stopped the water.

"You need to leave," she said, her voice low but fierce.

I looked around the room, making sense of my surroundings. Soft light penetrated the thin curtains in front of the glass doors of the deck. I didn't remember coming home, though I assumed I crashed on the couch so as not to disturb Laurie and also not to alert her to my state. That didn't work out so well. I did remember waking up with a coughing fit at some point and resuming sleep from an upright position. My shoes were splayed across the floor and a pack of smokes was on the coffee table. "What?" I asked pathetically. "What'd I do?"

Laurie rolled her eyes and contorted her face into the exasperation a parent might have with a wayward teen. "You can't come home like this," she said. "What if Josie had come out here first?" She passed her hand over my sorry state of being and the pack of smokes on the table. We didn't have to recognize that I reeked like the bars we used to frequent when booze spilled and people smoked inside.

"It wouldn't be the end of the world," I offered, desperate for some reprieve. "Kids see worse every day."

"That's not the point, you fucking asshole," she hissed, lunging over the counter. "She can't see you like this. She will not forget."

I wanted to blow off Laurie's words as hysteria, as overly protective, as PC bullshit, but I knew she was right. And I knew she knew drunks. It was her family business, where she had spent her childhood playing and her teens working. Her tolerance was low for the ugliness of alcohol. She'd seen it from a young age and did not wish the same upon her child as it can be confusing and scary to see an adult, a parent no less, in such a state. Something told me that I'd gotten off easy, that this could have been or would get worse if I didn't change course. In a way, in the parlance of bartenders, she was cutting me off.

"Go to Queens," Laurie said with compassionate authority. "Take some time to figure out what is going on with you. Think about getting some help, if that's what you need. We will be here for you, for whatever you need, but you have to go now."

"What will you tell Josie?" I asked in a tone that hoped to convey contrition as opposed to the actual humiliation.

"I'll tell her something," she said. "Don't worry about it."

"When will I be back?" I asked with a half-smile, hiding the horror that underpinned the question.

"I don't know, Andrew," Laurie said, looking away and then looking back at me. "When will you be back?"

I surveyed the room where my shame lingered like the awful taste in my mouth. Laurie threw me a kitchen towel, and I dried my hair and neck and face. "OK," I said, tossing the wet towel on the counter.

"Look," Laurie said, like the only adult in the room. "You can hit rock bottom, if that's what you're after. You just can't do it here."

I slipped on my shoes and walked out the door.

• • •

I called in sick to work from the corner and then hid out in a nearby coffee shop until the schoolyard began to empty. As the kids funneled inside, I fought the urge to catch a peek at Josie as she entered the building. I didn't deserve to see her, I thought, and I didn't want that to be the last image I had of her before my expulsion from home. I slipped up the street to get some things from the house before going to Queens. Tina was outside, watering the botanical gardens she kept in front.

She was dressed nice, like a lot of Italians do, even when watering the plants. Tina was no house-dress housewife, and I liked that about her, though she still had the instincts of the Old World women who seemed to know things without being told.

"Andrew," she sang in a tone that I found less than sincere. "How are you?"

"I'm fine, Tina," I lied. "How are you?"

"Not bad," she said, turning her hose back on to her plants. "Can't complain."

"That's good," I said and took the steps two at a time.

"Your wife just passed by with that gorgeous baby," she said as I worked the key in the lock. "What a beautiful family you have."

"Thanks," I said and hurried inside.

• • •

I felt like an intruder entering my own home, tiptoeing around, touching as little as possible as I

94

cleaned up and changed, and then packed clothes and toiletries in a suitcase. I put my laptop and school materials in a leather messenger briefcase Laurie had bought me as a present when I finished graduate school. Exhaustion has its limits, and I refused to feel anything and focused on getting myself out of the apartment because I knew that was the most productive thing I could do at the moment.

I remained in a trance-like state as I dragged my sorry ass out of the apartment and around the corner to the subway. I didn't deserve a taxi ride, and besides, at that hour, a taxi from Brooklyn to Queens would take even longer than the subway and, therefore, cost a small fortune. I took the train away from the city, toward the airport, and I was essentially alone in every car, my things around me as the trains rattled and rose above ground and then back under. It took three transfers and nearly two hours to go the long way from Brooklyn to Queens, but it was worth avoiding rush hour crowds and traffic.

When I descended the elevated stop in Queens, and walked the surrounding streets, the sounds and smells of the familiar neighborhood barely registered. I pulled the suitcase along and walked in a coma of detachment. I felt in between the lines of life, existing in a state of suspended emotion. My only motivation was to get from Point A (home in Brooklyn) to Point B (my temporary home in Queens) without complication. I knew all along that I had much unpleasantness to deal with, but the pause from perseveration — the constant wrestling with my state of being — felt like a small blessing. I also sensed, somewhere in the fringes of my consciousness that were actually working, that this return home, shame aside, had a purpose.

As I got closer to the neighborhood's center, a stronger sense of familiarity arrived. I recognized the routines, the sensory soundtrack of an album I'd heard a thousand times. I didn't miss the old neighborhood, though I was happy to have grown up there, for the privilege of being looked after and free at the same time. The pang of nostalgia turned into a pang of hunger, as I felt my senses coming back. It was mid-morning, quiet with the gentle sun bouncing off the car windows and a hush to the streets in the pause between the morning bustle and the day's first break. It was Friday, which felt like luck, since I didn't have to worry about work tomorrow and, more importantly considering my fledgling hunger, roast pork sandwiches were being made at the latticini across the street from my old house.

Our place was a two-story A-frame, in a row of similar houses, with brick on the first floor and aluminum siding up top. It was very Queens, this mid-century housing built with immigrants in mind, where families shared multi-unit buildings. I entered the small plot up-front through a low, wrought-iron gate and took the concrete steps to the staircase that led to the portico and the front door. I stowed my belongings behind the metal furniture and went back to the street, where I crossed, with my eyes on the Italian grocery that had fed me more than any other source other than my mother and grandmother.

I smelled the roasting pork before entering the empty storefront. Very little had changed, and it resembled the typical Italian groceries found throughout the city—canned and jarred goods, packaged pastas on the shelves and dried items, mostly meats and cheeses, hung from the ceiling above the display counters stuffed with more products and pastries. Fresh-baked breads in baskets. Italian nostalgia hung all over the walls. Typical, I guess, to other shops around the city and every Italian-American enclave in the country, but this place was special, not just because it was across the street from where I grew up, but because the three spinster sisters who ran Vito's Latticini (named after their father) loved people unconditionally, and it was expressed not only in their warmth but also in their food.

I stood in the empty storefront absorbing the aroma that had me swallowing the saliva conjured from my jowls and relishing the comforting memories swirling around my head. The reality of food provided a great sense of joy to me at the moment, and all I wanted to eat, more than anything else imaginable, was a roast pork sandwich on a long, semolina roll, topped with fresh mozzarella and roasted red peppers, a bag of sour cream and onion potato chips and a bottle of seltzer water. This was my go-to meal as a growing teenager, and one that had an important place in the menu of my life.

Finally, noise emanated from the back and through the swinging doors appeared sister Maria with an apron around her waist and a hairnet over her head. All three sisters were slender and ageless, close in age and equal in beauty. One of the whispered mysteries of the neighborhood was why none of them had ever married, but their privacy was ultimately respected since the food was so good and they were so kind.

"*Ann-Deee*," sister Maria sang in her accented, singsong way, taking twice as long to say my name as anyone else. "What brings you home?"

She pulled off her hairnet and came around the counter to take my face in her hands, which she inspected for a minute before pecking me hard on each cheek. I felt ashamed to be so close to someone while in such a state, and I suspected her concern at my compromised condition, even though I cleaned up as best I could before leaving home in a hurry.

"Ciao, Maria," I said, trying to be casual while coming up with a lie. "We're going to rent the upstairs, so I'm here for a little while to fix it up."

"Oh," she said, swiveling on a hip and twisting her head to consider my words. "OK."

Sister Maria had called bullshit on me with her nearly silent implication, but that was fine. I had other concerns, not the least of which was something to eat. "Is that the roast pork I'm smelling?" I asked.

"Yes, it is," she said with a little smile. "You want it same as always?"

I nodded and apologized with my eyes. She forgave me with a flat smile and returned to the kitchen after giving my forearm a quick clutch. As I waited for the food, competing emotions of shame and relief coursed through me, leaving me defeated and uplifted at the same time. I was embarrassed to be back home, to have to lie about the reasons, but it felt good to be there, too, like it was where I should be. That was one of the strange things about life since Mike had gotten sick and especially since he'd passed: It no longer felt like there was anyplace I belonged.

I looked out the storefront window, through the display and the etching on the glass, as the neighborhood passed, cars and pedestrians, and I thought of all the times I'd walked or run by or crossed from the corner coming from home, the sound the door made when it opened or closed, a little ding from a bell that said hello or goodbye.

I remembered how excited Mike would be, when we were teenagers, to take our food back across the street and eat on my porch, how he would claim, almost every time, once removing the paper wrapping and allowing the aroma to waft, that he was tempted to rub the warm contents on his chest before devouring it. I huffed a little laugh as I stood inside the doorway waiting for my lunch that day, shaking my head at the absurdity of Mike's statement but how it was so quintessentially him — somehow conveying his enthusiasm in a way that he would only share with me.

"Here you go," sister Maria said, her voice startling me from my memories.

She had the tubular sandwich wrapped tight in butcher's paper and held up like a prize. She placed it on the counter and put up her hand, instructing me to wait. I stared at the sandwich like a dog in a cartoon, enjoying the sense of silliness to it all, of something so pleasurable and simple causing consternation. I distracted myself by grabbing some chips from a rack and a bottle of seltzer from the refrigerated display case. When I got back to the counter, sister Maria was packing the sandwich into a large, cardboard box that was stuffed with groceries.

"What's this?" I asked.

"You're gonna be home for a bit," she said with a shrug. "Figured you'd need some food."

We exchanged looks for a moment, communicating things that had not been said.

"You gotta eat, right?" she broke our silence by saying.

I reached for my wallet, but she waved me off and pushed the box toward me. I picked it up. "I'm sorry about your friend, Andy," she said. "I truly am."

• • • •

I carried the bounty home and sat on the porch. I ate half the huge sandwich and wrapped the rest up for later. On separate trips, I brought the groceries and my belongings upstairs, after knocking on the door at the end of the dark hallway on the parlor floor, letting the mother of the family know I'd be upstairs. She didn't ask how long I'd be there, and I was glad because I didn't know myself, though I hoped upon hope that sister Maria had packed me too much food.

The upstairs apartment, a one bedroom floor-through, opened into a small hallway that fed into a threshold bordered by a bath, bedroom, and the kitchen with linoleum floors and the same appliances that my grandmother used every day of her entire life in America. I used to love running up the stairs, drawn by the smells from her cooking, sitting at the same round, wooden table that was still there, tasting sauce off the wooden spoon she carefully held to my lips that, upon my approval, would top spaghetti with meatballs and sausage, a lamb shank on good days, or my favorite: manicotti—her handmade crepes filled with fresh ricotta and gently baked.

After the sensory excursion down memory lane, I mindlessly stored my clothes away and put sheets on the bed. I opened the windows that looked over the small backyard that still held the fig tree my grandfather had planted. After opening the windows that faced the street, in the carpeted living room that featured the garish sofa across from the monster television console bookended by ornate sitting chairs, I returned to the kitchen and unpacked the generous grocery sack. Sister Maria had provided all the basics of an Italian kitchen: pasta, meats, cheeses, olive oil, garlic, pureed tomatoes, eggs, bread and bread crumbs. "You gotta eat," I heard her say in my head, and the thought filled me with comfort, as did her generosity and concern.

It was barely past noon, but I suddenly felt very, very tired, not just from the night before and the events of the morning, but tired from everything. I plopped on the couch, closed my eyes and fell fast asleep. I had no dreams, and I woke slicked with sweat under my chin on the front of my neck. It was 4:00, and I wondered who was taking care of Josie after school, if Laurie had stayed home or found a sitter. I missed my daughter but sensed that I was in the right place at the moment. I also knew she was in good hands and that I only had to worry about myself for a little while so I could get back to my lovely family.

• • •

I took a long, hot shower and put on fresh clothes, a typical childhood getup of jeans, T-shirt, sneakers and a hoodie. I bounded down the familiar steps to the street and unlatched the gate. I looked in both directions, instinctively searching for friends, and then walked toward Mike's house. The sun, just starting to descend, threw slanted sunlight that made long shadows from the cherry trees that had recently bloomed, the slight breeze making confetti out of their petals. I turned the corner on Mike's block and stood in front of his house, resisting the urge to walk up and knock, just for the indulgence in a familiar practice.

I imagined an eight-year-old Mike coming out the door and down the steps, across the area in front, where his mother and my mother used to sit on a wooden bench while Mike and I, as toddlers, would push trucks around the slate surface. A 12-year-old Mike came out of the gate and met me on the street with an open palm that awaited my fist; we walked toward the schoolyard to look for other kids, to assess the happenings, our fingers latched onto the cyclone fence, our noses up against the speckled iron.

"Come on, And," a fifteen-year-old Mike said to me. We walked away from the schoolyard and toward the commercial center of the neighborhood, where the two roads that intersected were lined with storefronts for blocks in all four directions. We passed on the pizzeria as it was too close to dinnertime and we didn't want to get in trouble with our moms, so we had an Italian Ice (cherry for Mike, rocket pop for me) out front of the Italian Ice stand and watched the girls our age walk by, their new spring clothes fluttered by the breeze.

I went to Brady's alone, abandoning my imaginary walk with Mike, though he was waiting for me, sort of, behind the bar in a photograph, a formal shot in full FDNY regalia, metal-framed and hung right next to the register. I thought of the summer Mike and I turned 21, and we'd meet most nights at Brady's for a few beers. Mike was in the firefighter's academy and still living at home; I was back from college, working in the manufacturing facility for my father, doing odd jobs in the back of the plant. We'd get there around the same time, straight from our respective daytime obligations. It felt adult-like, to enter a bar without pause, to nod at the regulars and wave to the tender, to assume a regular spot. The spot for me and Mike back then was around the bend at the far end of the bar, a dark corner compared to the areas up front where the regulars drank in the better light, in the heart of the action.

Everyone knew Mike at the bar as his extended family had been regulars for generations. We were allowed in there as kids, to run around, drink sodas and watch the Mets or the Jets on TV, but we were forbidden from sitting at the bar. Once we were legal, it felt like a rite of passage to pop into Brady's, take a stool and have a few belts. Mike would get his first bartending job there, the summer after we turned 21 and he was accepted into the FDNY, but that previous summer, as meaningful as it seemed to me, was not particularly special to Mike nor pleasant. He was struggling with some of the academic aspects of the academy, so we'd spend our time at the bar not shooting the shit, like everyone else in the joint, but talking through some of the challenges he faced unpacking the best practices and procedures required of New York City firefighters. "Thanks," he'd say sincerely to me once we had cleared up the confusion over a couple of beers and he had asked for the tab. "I got these, Professor."

On the first day of my exile back home in Queens, sitting at the bar in the company of Mike's framed photo, I laughed to myself, thinking of his prescience in calling me "Professor" all those years ago. He knew before anyone else, it seemed, that storytelling and teaching were my calling. He knew me better than anybody else ever had or ever would. And that point began to resonate as I sat at the bar and stared at Mike's image just as another moment of illumination was about to arrive.

• • •

"How's it going there, Andy?" Bones Malone asked from behind the bar.

The bar's ownership changed hands all the time, usually a group of locals who bought it together to keep the joint from going out of business when the existing owners no longer wanted the hassle of running a dilapidated watering hole with minimal profit margin. It was more like community service than entrepreneurship. Bones Malone, a neighborhood guy and a day trader on the floor of the New York Stock Exchange, was one of the current owners. He was older than us by a few years, and he had a look that Mike would describe as "the map of Ireland on his face" — fair hair and skin, the latter tinged with pink, bright eyes of gray and blue, sharp angles for cheeks and chin.

"Hey, Bones," I said. "How are you?"

He looked at Mike's picture and then back at me. "Doing OK," he said. "How 'bout yourself?"

I shrugged and tried to make a brave face, thinking that the crowd in Brady's was not going to cut me any sympathy slack, but Bones leaned closer to me, his hands on the bar, his knowing Irish eyes sparkling and sad and kind. "You remember Kenny Gilligan, don't you?"

I nodded. Kenny Gilligan was a kid, even older than Bones, who had been hit by a car and killed when I was about eight or nine years old. I recalled the story of him and his friends running from an electronics store where they had shoplifted a stereo, the owner hot on their trail, and Kenny Gilligan cutting between cars, crossing the busy boulevard without looking first, where he was struck and killed by a delivery truck. I hadn't thought of Kenny Gilligan in a long time, and I held Bones' eyes and wondered why he brought it up.

"My cousin Blaise was best friends with Kenny their whole lives growing up," he said quietly. "And his death, right, messed up Blaise real bad."

"I bet," I said, trying to make simple sense of what I had just been told. "You can't un-see that."

"No," Bones said, leaning closer and practically whispering. "He wasn't even there that day when it happened, but the death, the absence, I guess, of his friend messed him up for a lot of years. It took therapy, years down the road, for him to figure it out."

"Wow," I said. "That's pretty heavy."

"That's what I'm saying," Bones Malone said to me from behind the bar at Brady's. "Now what can I get ya?"

I drank some beers alone at Brady's, and then the place started to fill up, so I drank a few more with guys I knew from the neighborhood and some of the old-timers. It felt good to be in their collective warmth, but I had no plans of staying too long. Dinnertime approached, and the food at Brady's was worse than the decor. On Fridays and Saturdays they had a horrible buffet in the back room, featuring boiled hot dogs that were served on generic buns piled on a platter. There was a hot plate and some large serving pans over water trays, usually filled with something someone made at home, like corned beef or meatloaf or shepherd's pie. All of it was awful Irish fare, as far as I was concerned, though the bar patrons, full of booze and not of particular palates, gobbled it all up.

I walked outside into the last remnants of daylight, my eyes adjusting to the slightly brighter environs, and air that didn't smell of beer-soaked floors and beer-soaked men. The sky faded into a midnight-blue blanket as I walked the avenue toward home at dusk, the early evening rush blurring past my morning pace. I had a pretty good buzz going, but it was noticeably less than that brought on by the Big Gulp martinis I'd been having each evening before dinner. My desire to prepare and eat food was in place, so I picked up a bottle of Italian red and resumed my stroll home.

Lights glowed from above the street and in front of the homes on my block. It reminded me of when

I was young, coming home at this hour for dinner, not having a curfew of a particular time but "when the lights came on." I entered the yard and climbed the stairs, knowing all along what I was going to make for dinner. The foyer was dimly lit, and the stairwell upstairs was nearly dark, but I recalled the familiarity of each step as I climbed up and found the switch that provided light.

The inside of the small apartment was cool, and I closed the windows in front and back and then got to work in the well-lit kitchen. The sink faced the small alley between our building and the neighbor's, and on the windowsill was a small transistor radio that my grandmother always had on, listening to her favorite DJ, William B. Williams, spin Sinatra songs and those from the other crooners she adored. I turned it on, and the jazz station out of Jersey played, indicating that my father had been the last one to tune the radio, probably while doing some work upstairs after my grandmother had passed.

It was her recipe that I followed that night, the first dish she had ever taught me to make: pasta aglio e olio, which translated simply into pasta with garlic and oil. As the harmony of horns and rhythm sections filtered through the kitchen, I put on a pot of water to boil and then began mincing garlic cloves, separated and peeled, from the bulb sister Maria had provided in her care package. The cupboards still held basics, like salt and dried herbs and different peppers. There were even some anchovies packed in salt and oil, along with sardines in cans. I washed and dried the largest sauté pan and put it on the front burner on medium heat, where the mound of minced garlic began to gently brown in a bath of olive oil. I turned off the heat before the garlic burned and added some red pepper flakes. I did all of this, like climbing darkened stairs, by instinct, in a cocoon of familiarity and comfort.

When the water began to boil, I salted it generously, always remembering my grandmother's instruction to "make it taste like the ocean." I popped open the wine and poured some into one of the juice glasses from the cupboard, not wondering why my parents had left the apartment intact for so many years but happy they had done so, almost as if it were waiting for me. It wasn't, I knew, but I acted as if it were while I set two places at the wooden table and prepared to finish the pasta. I transferred the nearly al dente spaghetti from the water directly into the pan now back on the burner at medium heat. I turned the pasta over and over in the garlic and oil, allowing it to finish cooking and absorb the flavors. Off the heat, I gave the pasta a swirl of fresh olive oil and a serious sprinkle of grated Pecorino Romano. I turned the pasta again and took it to the table where I plated a fourth of the pasta onto my plate and the rest on Mikey's.

Aglio e olio was not my favorite pasta dish, nor was it Mike's (he was a rigatoni and meat sauce man; I preferred linguine with seafood fra diavolo), but it was what I made us when we, as late-teens and young adults, came home in the wee hours after a night of partying. "Come on, And," Mike would implore. "Let's have a little something."

That "little something" would be a full pound of pasta made in my parents' kitchen, the quantity doled out heavily in Mike's favor, a quick and filling meal to absorb the alcohol and provide an extension to the exploits of two old friends.

Watching Mike eat, especially at that hour, was something to behold. There were no words, just sounds of consumption and indications of approval. He'd hover over his plate and funnel the food with a fork into his mouth seemingly without pause. "Why don't you just bob for it?" I'd ask sardonically on occasion. Mike would turn his head and hold my eye for a moment, a bemused smile tempting the sides of his mouth before his eyes would return to blank and he'd turn his attention back to his food. It reminded me of the singularly-focused eating habits of a shark.

When he was done, Mike would push back his chair, take the plate to the sink, and make for the door. "Catch ya later, And," he said on his way out.

I ate my pasta aglio e olio alone that night in my grandmother's apartment. The simplicity and balance of the dish, not to mention the nostalgia it conjured, filled me with well-being. I didn't imagine Mike there, as I'd been doing all day, but I felt connected to him nonetheless in a profound way. The wine washed away the mouth feel of the pasta, and each new bite felt like a rebirth. Finding solace in food delivered a blessing, and I sensed the communion with my friend on a spiritual level.

When I was done, I sat at the table and sipped some wine. I put the cork back in the half-finished bottle and set the oven to 375 degrees. I scraped Mike's full plate of pasta into a large, stainless steel bowl. In another bowl I cracked six eggs and whipped them with grated cheese. I put on the burner under the same pan, still coated in oil, and added the eggs and cheese to the bowl full of pasta. Mixing the pasta with the cheese and eggs made me smile.

It was almost bedtime for Josie on a non-school night, and I decided to call just before 9:00, as she was surely finishing up a Disney movie or a *Kim Possible* episode with Laurie. I couldn't wait to hear her voice and let her know that I was about to make her favorite pasta dish: spaghetti pie.

I slept well, alone in the quiet apartment, relieved to be removed from a routine that in many ways I had made grueling through torpor and avoidance. Well-rested and thinking somewhat clearly, for a change,

I made espresso in an old aluminum pot and cut a slice of spaghetti pie from the plate upon which I had left it covered in foil overnight. As I had my breakfast at the kitchen table, I thought of the loose definition of "insanity" as doing the same thing over and over and expecting a different result. Then I thought of Cher smacking Nicolas Cage across the face in the movie *Moonstruck* then ordering him to "Snap out of it!" As if breaking from one's absurd tendencies was that easy.

The buzzer in the apartment rang, jarring me from my thoughts like a slap from Cher. The speaker was on the interior wall beside the kitchen's entrance, and it made a harsh, abrupt tone, as if someone had gotten an answer wrong on a game show. I was startled as much by the sound as the thought of who it could be. There was no intercom, only the ability to be notified that someone was on the porch. I walked to the speaker and looked at it as if clues were inside the slated plastic interface. I hurried into the bedroom to change from my pajamas.

The buzzer rang again before I could get out of the apartment door, and I yelled, "Coming!" as I paddled down the stairs, though I knew I could not be heard down the long hallway and through the thick door. Dull light bloomed through the small, fogged window in the front door. The back of a figure could be made out, sitting on the steps, facing the street. I opened the door and discovered my friend Bill, dressed in tennis gear, two rackets in their protective cases and a knapsack at his side. He twisted his torso and said with a smile, "Hey, Pal. I thought you weren't home, so I was fixing to wait."

My friend and former neighbor stood and approached to give me a clasped handshake and a firm pat on my shoulder. He looked with compassion into my face, and I enjoyed the warmth of his glance and the kindness of his unexpected gesture. The joy of Bill's presence was belied somewhat by the guilt I felt for not returning the many calls he had made to me over the past few months. "Hey, man," I said, baffled but happy. "What the hell?"

"Oh, you know," he said, looking back at the street. "I was just rolling through Queens, looking for a tennis match. I heard there are some players out here."

"Shit," I said solemnly, thinking how out of practice I was. "You might want to look a little harder."

Bill laughed before his face went serious. "Come on, man," he said. "Go get dressed. I got everything else you need."

I took a deep breath and nodded in agreement, but then quickly changed my countenance, too. "How'd you find me?"

Bill clucked his tongue and nodded. "Laurie called me up, said you might need some company."

I looked over Bill's shoulder, focused on the sun spangling off the windshields of the passing traffic. Whatever embarrassment I might have felt about Laurie's intervention was buried under a mountain of gratitude. "You want to come in?" I asked.

"Nah," he said. "I'm good right here."

He returned to the steps, leaned back on his forearms and stretched out like a cat in the sun.

"OK," I said. "I'll be right back."

· · ·

Bill kicked my ass in tennis in all three sets and then dropped me off back home in Queens. I had tried to lure him in for lunch with the promise of half a roast pork sandwich and/or spaghetti pie, but he had to get back to Brooklyn for an afternoon gig. I sat on the stoop in the warmth of the sun. I was tired but exhilarated by the exercise, concentration and competition. The companionship had also bolstered my spirits, and Bill and I played hard against each other but did so in the good faith of friendship. I wanted to win, he wanted to win, but we both wanted to enjoy each other's company. We had, and I was so grateful that Laurie had called Bill and that Bill was my friend.

It was there in that moment, reflecting on the familiar yet profound value of friendship, that clarity regarding Mike's loss kindly arrived like the sunshine warming my arms and face: Mike knew me better than anyone else ever had or ever would. We spent so much time together growing up, so immersed in the magic of childhood, so engaged in the wonder of exploration and adventure, so connected by ritual and shared space and secrets, it was like our DNA had merged: spit and blood and sweat. Baptism water. Maybe it was also all the soda cans and candy bars and Italian Ices we passed back and forth; the beds and back seats and bike seats we shared; the balls we threw to each other in the street or in the schoolyard; the same asphalt and sidewalks that tore our elbows and knees; the same air we breathed in and out; the arms we threw naturally around each other's shoulders; the thousands of times I popped my fist into his palm. And these rituals, our communion, continued into adolescence and adulthood.

Mike was part of my whole life. And then he wasn't. Out of habit, honed over a lifetime, I kept looking for Mike but he was no longer there. Mike was like my right-hand man, the first person I turned to whenever life summoned the need for the inclusion of another. And almost like someone who literally loses their right hand, I kept looking to that place where the hand once was, unable to undo the attachment. The recurring void was filled by sorrow, and this sorrow is a place of which one can't be prepared. You can only know it when you get there, and knowing it—and knowing that it has been earned, and knowing it is something you'd never trade in a million years—is the start of celebrating the life of a lost one as opposed to mourning it.

I went inside and took a shower. I called Laurie and got her voicemail; I left a message asking for her and Josie to please meet me at Brady's at 6:00. I didn't explain why, but I sensed that the tone of my voice would imply the good nature of the request. Then I put all the groceries sister Maria had gifted me on the counter and got to work making dinner in honor of Pasta Mike.

• • •

By 5:30 everything was done. There was nothing left to cook, and enough Italian food to feed the patrons of an Irish bar after Happy Hour on a Saturday night. While out to get some large aluminum tins, I'd stopped by Brady's and expressed to Bones Malone my desire to cater that night's dinner and pay tribute to Mike. "Brilliant, Andy," he said. "We didn't have a proper salute of just the neighborhood anyway. Mind if I make a few calls to spread the word?"

"Not at all," I said and went home to start packing up the food after picking up a few more pounds of pasta and more ingredients from the latticini across the street. The aging afternoon was cool and cloudless, the sky deep and blue and serene. As I crossed the street, my phone vibrated in my pocket. The call must have come in when I was in the latticini, talking to the sisters. I sat on the stoop and accessed the voicemail. "Hello, Daddy," Josie's singsong voice chimed. "Me and Mama was at a birthday party."

Her "hello" sounded like "heh-woa" and her "party" sounded like "pah-tee" and the adorable pronunciations of my adorable child filled me with joy, as did the words that followed, dictated to her by her mother and my wife. "Mama says we're coming to Queens."

Back upstairs, I filled the tins with the sauces that would dress the pounds of rigatoni made at the bar in the giant pot usually used for boiling hot dogs. I'd also made lasagna in the biggest pan of my grandmother's arsenal. I carefully carried two trays at a time down the stairs and out of the gate, along the familiar route to Brady's. Thoughts of my grandmother and Mike surrounded me as I considered their special bond, of how much she loved feeding Mike and how much he loved to be fed by her. I loved both of them and knew that their bond, in part, was based on their mutual affection for me.

The barroom was already half-full when I arrived with the first trays around 5:30. Bones waved to me from behind the bar and pointed to the back room where the water trays had been set up with the flames ignited beneath. I put my trays in and headed back through the barroom, where I refused multiple offers for a drink. I felt more electric and alive than I had in a very long time.

Shadows extended across the streets and sidewalks as I hurried back home for the final set of trays. The avenues teemed with the energy of a lovely Saturday afternoon fading into evening. People were dressed for dinner, and I imagined the restaurants of the neighborhood crowded and echoing with celebration. It felt like the whole world would be out that night, though most of them didn't know that arguably the most meaningful celebration for so many, and especially for me, would be had at Brady's Irish Haven.

• •

The barroom was full but not too full. Unlike the Irish wake, there was space to move and socialize without having to yell to be heard. Most importantly, those not at the bar or with access to some of the makeshift seating would be able to eat standing up. The crowd varied in age but was mostly the old-timers and the many people Mike and I had grown up with. Some of Mike's cousins, who still lived around, were there as well as faces unfamiliar to me, who were either new to the neighborhood or friends of friends. The vibe was festive and inclusive. Bones Malone called me over, and I met him across the nicked mahogany once I delivered the final trays in back.

"Well done there, Andy," he said. "We should do this every Saturday."

"Maybe we should," I suggested.

"Are you serious?" he asked.

"Why not?" I answered. "Mike would love it."

Bones looked around his barroom, crowded and festive early on a Saturday night. "All right, then," he said with a nod. "We'll call it Pasta Night."

"Let's go with Pasta Mike," I suggested.

Bones looked at me quizzically and nodded again. "If you wish."

"You mind if I make a toast, once my wife and daughter arrive?"

"Not at all," he said. "Now what can I get ya?"

I ordered a Smithwick and sipped it alone, studying Mike's face in the framed photo behind the bar. From the angle, it looked as if he were smiling. I realized that he would have hated how I reacted to his death, how I had allowed it to adversely affect my life. There was an aspect to our friendship, a guardianship of him upon me, in which I was to be protected at all costs. The idea of him actually causing me pain was too much to bear.

Once, when we were in high school, we were messing around in the back of the pizza place, trying to impress some girls our age. Mike made the girls laugh with a joke at my expense, so I shoved him playfully. This was when he had just started lifting weights seriously and, unaware of his new strength, he shoved me back. I flew across the room and hit the side of my head on the corner of a table. Mike ran over and helped me up. "And. And," he asked frantically. "You OK? You OK?"

I was holding the side of my head with one hand. When I pulled it away, my fingers were covered in blood. One of the girls screamed. Mike began to cry. And he continued to cry as the pizzeria owner led me out of the shop and into his delivery car for a trip to the hospital for stitches. Mike sat with me in the back of the car and continued to cry and apologize until I asked him with great animation, "Who's the one bleeding here?"

We laughed about that all the time. It was one of our recurring lines from a lifetime of stories together. I touched the scar underneath my hairline as I stared at Mike's picture at Brady's. I vowed to not make him cry.

"Here's your wife and kid now," Bones' voice interrupting my communion with Mike. Laurie's upper torso crossed the threshold of the bar and worked through the crowd. The top of Josie's head appeared in glimpses in front of her mother. I waved to get Laurie's attention. She smiled, bent forward and pointed in my direction. Bodies jostled as an invisible figure cut a path in my direction and appeared like an apparition between the nearby bodies.

"Daddy!" Josie squealed and leapt into my arms. "Are you OK? Are you OK?"

I hugged her tiny frame and closed my eyes, remembering when Mike had asked me the same thing. When I opened my eyes, Laurie was in front of me. "Hey," she said, and touched one of my arms that held our daughter tight.

I put Josie down. "Hey," I said back to her. "Thanks for coming."

"Wouldn't miss it," she said.

A hand grabbed my shoulder from behind, and I turned to the bar. "We should probably get started here with the food," Bones said to me, after he nodded to Laurie and Josie. "Did you want to say a few words first?"

"I do," I said.

"Well, come on then," he said, motioning to the bar top.

The drinkers to my side made room per Bones' request, and I used a stool to climb up on the bar, where all eyes soon turned to me. A ceiling fan across the room was level with the top of my head, and the room seemed so vast from this vantage point.

"Quiet now. Quiet now," Bones yelled to the room. "This man has something to say."

I looked around, at the faces familiar and unknown, at my wife and my daughter, and finally, for a moment, at the framed photo of my oldest friend.

"Let me tell you the story of Pasta Mike," I began.

THE END

ABOUT THE AUTHOR

Andrew Cotto is an award-winning novelist and a regular contributor to *The New York Times*. He has also written for *La Cucina Italiana, Brooklyn Magazine, The Good Men Project, Rachael Ray In Season, Parade, Men's Journal, Rolling Stone, Condé Nast Traveler, Italy Magazine, AARP,* and more. Andrew has an MFA in Creative Writing from The New School. He lives in Brooklyn, NY.

NOTE FROM THE AUTHOR

Word-of-mouth is crucial for any author to succeed. If you enjoyed *Pasta Mike*, please leave a review online — anywhere you are able. Even if it's just a sentence or two. It would make all the difference and would be very much appreciated.

Thanks!
Andrew Cotto

We hope you enjoyed reading this title from:

BLACK ROSE
writing™

www.blackrosewriting.com

Subscribe to our mailing list—*The Rosevine*—and receive **FREE** books, daily deals, and stay current with news about upcoming releases and our hottest authors.

Scan the QR code below to sign up.

Already a subscriber? Please accept a sincere thank you for being a fan of Black Rose Writing authors.

View other Black Rose Writing titles at www.blackrosewriting.com/books and use promo code **PRINT** to receive a **20% discount** when purchasing.